Stories Told by 'Abdu'l-Bahá

STORIES TOLD
BY
'ABDU'L-BAHÁ

compiled by

Amir Badiei

George Ronald
Oxford

George Ronald, *Publisher*
46 High Street, Kidlington, Oxford OX5 2DN

A catalogue record for this book is available from the British Library

ISBN 0–85398–484–0

Contents

CONTENTS

CONTENTS

This book is dedicated to the memory of my late father

Muhammad Badiei

who was a treasure house of stories

and who related to my siblings and myself numerous stories

several of which appear in this volume

Preface

During the past one hundred years or so there have been many people who have written or told stories about 'Abdu'l-Bahá. It is indeed a blessing to have access to these accounts about the Christ-like life of one who is the Perfect Exemplar of the teachings of Bahá'u'lláh and whose way of life provides a noble example for all to follow. Generations to come will be eternally grateful to those people of foresight who have left to posterity such a priceless gift.

The stories presented in this compilation, however, are not about 'Abdu'l-Bahá – they are written or told by Him. In His writings and in His talks, formal or informal, 'Abdu'l-Bahá used stories to explain to His readers or audiences the principles of the Faith, to clarify for them a topic, to help them find meaning in their lives, to acquaint them with some religious and historical people and episodes, to warn them against the harmful activities of the enemies of the Faith, to remind them of the saintly lives of some of the early believers and to entertain them. However, separated from the context of His writings or speeches, some of the stories might not convey the same message for which they were originally told. Story 105, for example, was related by Him while advising the friends to cooperate and help each other with their teaching work. Stripped of His talk the story fails to communicate this message and tells only of an interesting event. To lessen the effect of this omission, a short description of 'Abdu'l-Bahá's topic of discussion has been added at the end of some of the stories.

The beauty and significance of some of these stories have also been adversely impacted by their translation into the English language. By the very nature of its development, a folk story is closely tied to the culture and language of the people of the land where it originated. Such a story will lose much of its charm and subtlety if removed from its original culture and told in a foreign tongue. For this reason a few stories, which could not retain their import in their translated version, were excluded from the present compilation. There are also numerous other stories told by 'Abdu'l-Bahá, or attributed to Him, which are not included in this compilation.

The reader might have heard different versions of these stories. In fact, 'Abdu'l-Bahá Himself has related some of them differently on different occasions. Stories are, after all, just stories. No one expects them to be quoted verbatim like a holy text. The message of each story remains the same, however, despite variation in its narration. It must also be mentioned here that a great number of 'Abdu'l-Bahá's stories are found exclusively in pilgrims' notes which are not to be regarded as an authentic source.

Many of the stories have been translated from their original Persian into English by the compiler. A good number of them were already translated by the early Persian Bahá'ís who came to the United States. Where such translations have been published, as in *Star of the West* or *The Promulgation of Universal Peace*, these translations have been used in the present volume.

'Abdu'l-Bahá liked to tell and to hear stories. While He was in the United States, a luncheon party was given in His honour by Mrs Agnes Parsons in Dublin, New Hampshire. In *Portals to Freedom* Howard Colby Ives writes,

> . . . the hostess made an opening, as she thought, for 'Abdu'l-Bahá to speak on spiritual things.
>
> His response to this was to ask if He might tell them a story; and He related one of the Oriental tales, of which He had a great store, and at its conclusion all laughed heartily.
>
> The ice was broken. Others added stories of which the Master's anecdote had reminded them. Then, 'Abdu'l-Bahá, His face beaming with happiness, told another story, and

another. His laughter rang through the room. He said that the Orientals had many such stories illustrating different phases of life. Many of them are extremely humorous. It is good to laugh. Laughter is a spiritual relaxation.*

People everywhere enjoy stories. For many years the compiler has been sharing these stories with friends and family. They have never failed to evoke in the audience a sense of appreciation, happiness and ease. This positive reception served as encouragement to present them in manuscript form for the benefit of all the friends. It is hoped that this collection will provide light and useful reading for everyone, especially children. The combination of each story with the sacred text that precedes it could be used effectively by parents and teachers for daily reading with children. Most of these stories told by 'Abdu'l-Bahá are factual and should prove refreshing in today's literature market, which is flooded with fictional tales of questionable quality.

No special order has been followed in the presentation of these stories. An attempt has been made, however, to place those which share a common element or a similar message one after the other.

* Ives, *Portals to Freedom*, pp. 119–20.

Introduction

Stories have always been important as means of illustrating principle, improving retention in learning and providing a way to meaningfully engage people of all ages. For Bahá'ís, what could be more helpful than a collection of stories told by 'Abdu'l-Bahá to illustrate the many points He wished to highlight in various talks and Tablets? This unique collection of stories related by the beloved Master in the course of His talks and correspondence is a first in the English-speaking world and provides a welcome addition to current Bahá'í literature. Ranging from light and humorous to serious and philosophical, the stories are bound to educate and delight the reader. Not only do they have an intrinsic value for the sheer joy of reading pleasure, the stories serve as an important and welcome addition to the materials needed for the growing numbers of people who are engaged in developing classes for all ages, as well as greatly enhancing the pool of source materials for an ever-expanding number of artistic pursuits. This volume will surely become a favourite for all ages!

Erica Toussaint
June 2003

Publisher's Note

Many of the stories contained in this book are found in sources such as *Star of the West*, *Abdul Baha in Egypt* and *The Light of the World*, published well before Shoghi Effendi standardized for Bahá'ís the spelling of the names of the Central Figures of the Faith, the word 'Bahá'í' and other terminology. The Publisher has taken the decision to reproduce the stories as they appear in these published sources, including the transliteration of names and places, so as not to change text inadvertently and thereby change meaning. It is recognized that this introduces an inconsistency into the text which we usually try to avoid but it was felt that on this occasion such inconsistency was acceptable.

In translations made directly from Persian, we have generally omitted the word 'Haḍrat', meaning 'His Holiness', before such names as Muḥammad. Translations of the words of Bahá'u'lláh and 'Abdu'l-Bahá where not from translations authorized by Shoghi Effendi or the Universal House of Justice are provisional.

Acknowledgements

I wish to express my thanks to my children, Daleer and Soha Badiei, for their encouragement and the continuity of their assistance throughout the whole period it took to prepare this manuscript.

I am most grateful to Julie Sutherland and Gail Alberini for the many hours they spent reviewing, correcting and typing these stories. Their joyful readiness to assist made my task much easier.

I am also grateful to the following publishers and copyright holders for permission to reprint or translate stories found in their publications:

Bahá'í Publications Australia and Andrew Gash for permission to reprint stories from Andrew Gash, *Stories from 'Star of the West'*, 1985.

Bahá'í Publishing Trust, New Delhi, for permission to translate stories from 'Abdu'l-Ḥamid-i Ishráq Khávarí, *Má'idiy-i-Ásmání*, 1984; and from 'Abdu'l-Ḥamid-i Ishráq Khávarí, *Payám-i-Malakút*, 1986.

Bahá'í-Verlag, Hofheim, for permission to translate stories from 'Abdu'l-Ḥamid-i Ishráq Khávarí, *Muḥáḍirát*, 1987; and from Ḥabíb Mu'ayyad, *Kháṭirát-i-Ḥabíb*, 1998.

Kalimát Press, Los Angeles, for permission to translate stories from Yúnis Afrúkhtih, *Kháṭirát-i Nuh Sálih*, 1983; and from *The Diary of Juliet Thompson*, 1983.

National Spiritual Assembly of the Bahá'ís of France and Dr Shapour Rassekh for permission to translate stories from *Payám-i-Ásmání*, 2001.

Oneworld Publications, Oxford, for permission to translate stories from Abu'l-Qásim Afnán, *'Ahd-i A'lá Zindigáníy-i Ḥaḍrat-i Báb*, 2000.

Dr Nossrat Pesechkian for permission to reprint a story from *The Merchant and the Parrot*, 1982.

This Witty Old Man Thought He Was Only 12 Years Old

'For service in love for mankind is unity with God. He who serves has already entered the Kingdom and is seated at the right hand of his Lord.'[1]

'Abdu'l-Bahá

A great king walking in his garden one day noticed a man, about ninety years old, planting some trees. The king asked what he was doing and the old man answered that he was planting date seeds. 'How long before they will bear fruit?' asked the king. 'Twenty years,' the old man answered. 'But you will not live to enjoy the fruit, why then should you plant these trees?' said the king. The man answered: 'The last generation planted trees that bore fruit for my benefit, so it is now my duty to plant for the benefit of the next generation.'

The king was pleased at this answer so gave the man a piece of money. The gardener fell on his knees and thanked him. The king asked, 'Why do you kneel before me?' 'Because, your majesty, not only have I had the pleasure or gift of planting these seeds but they have already borne fruit, since you gave me this money.' This so pleased the king he gave the man another piece of money.

Again the old gardener knelt, saying, 'Again I kneel to thank your majesty. Most trees will bear fruit only once, while these trees of mine have already borne two crops – since you give me two pieces of money.'

The king smiled and asked, 'How old are you?' The man answered, 'I am twelve years old.'

'How can that be, you are surely a very old man?' The gardener answered, 'In the days of the king your predecessor, the people were in a most unhappy state of constant warfare and trouble, so I cannot include that as part of my life. But since your majesty came to rule, the people are happy, contented and at peace. Therefore, as it is but twelve years since your gracious reign began, I am only twelve years old.' This pleased the king so much that, perforce, he gave the old man another piece of money, saying, 'I shall have to leave you now, for your words please me so greatly that if I listen to you longer I shall become a pauper!'[2]

One day in 'Akká a woman told 'Abdu'l-Bahá that she had been a Bahá'í for nine years and that she felt younger every day. He said that in reality she was only nine years old and then related this story.

2

The Pure-Hearted Baktáshí Died a Strange Death

'Be swift in the path of holiness, and enter the heaven of communion with Me. Cleanse thy heart with the burnish of the spirit, and hasten to the court of the Most High.'[3]
Bahá'u'lláh

Facing the house of Abdul Baha in Adrianople, there was a café. Here every day sat a retired officer of the Turkish Army belonging to the Baktashi's sect.[4] The Baktashis are always on good terms with the Bahais. They are a peaceful people. This retired soldier received a pension of 5 Piasters (25¢) a day from the government. Every morning he would come and take a chair in front of the café and order a cup of coffee. Then the people would gather around him and listen with delight and laughter to his stories until noon. At that hour he would call the waiter and give him five cents to buy him two loaves of bread, two rolls of roast-meat and a dish of salad. Then he would ask for a clean table and use his neat handkerchief as a tablecloth. Every day he invited one of the habitués of the café to lunch with him. 'Come here, my friend!' he would say, placing a chair on the other side of the table, and leaving before it a loaf of bread and one of the roast-meats. 'Come and be my guest today.' Then he would commence to eat. Every mouthful that was taken was followed by the short sentence 'Oh God! I thank Thee! How delicious is this lunch!' – till it was finished. Then again he would start his conversation, always tempered with sharp wit and the joy of living. From time to time he would come to the Mosque of Sultan Suleiman [Sulaymán] where the Governor and the officers would gather about him to pass a pleasant hour. He would keep them roaring with laughter over his stories. One day . . . the Baktashi entered with a mat under his arm. Laughingly he saluted everyone and said: 'Today I am going to start on a long journey; therefore, I beg you all to forgive all my past shortcomings!' 'Art thou going to Bagdad?' one asked. 'Further! much further!' 'Surely to China?' 'Very much further.' 'Then no doubt to Australia?' 'Still further.' All this time everybody laughed because they thought he had a joke up his sleeve. 'Please, please,' he pleaded, 'I beg you to forgive me. Say that you do!'

In order to humour him, they said, 'All right, we forgive thee!' Then he said: 'I am now happy. I also forgive you, my good friends.' Then he walked toward the court of the Mosque; spread on the ground half of his mat, laid himself down and covered his body with the other half. The spectators, thinking that they had reached the climax of the joke, laughed uproariously. Five minutes passed – no movement; ten, fifteen minutes, half an hour, no sign of life. The time grew heavy and strained. They looked at each other with wonder in their eyes. Then laughing and shrugging their shoulders, they left their places and gathered around the mat. One of them, on tip-toe, cautiously lifted one corner. Wonder of wonders! The Baktashi had breathed his last. Then these men carried him on their shoulders laughing and singing, took him to the undertaker laughing, washed his body laughing and buried him with roars and thunders of laughter. It was a most phenomenal event! This

3

Baktashi . . . knew something concerning the Cause. The believers asked him several times to call on the Blessed Perfection, but he always refused saying: 'How can I, the essence of sin, stand in the presence of the Essence of Holiness? I am not worthy of this privilege. Whenever I find that I deserve such honour, I will go; but not now, not now!' Thus this good man lived and died in happiness.[5]

We should try to live a good and happy life.

3

Nabíl Chose His Grave Site a Day Before His Death

'From the excellence of so great a Revelation the honour with which its faithful followers must needs be invested can be well imagined. By the righteousness of the one true God! The very breath of these souls is in itself richer than all the treasures of the earth.'[6]   Bahá'u'lláh

On a certain day, walking through the bázár with his friends, he [Nabíl of Qá'in[7]] met a gravedigger named Ḥájí Aḥmad. Although in the best of health, he addressed the gravedigger and laughingly told him: 'Come along with me.' Accompanied by the believers and the gravedigger, he made for Nabíyu'lláh Ṣáliḥ. Here he said, 'O Ḥájí Aḥmad, I have a request to make of you: when I move on, out of this world and into the next, dig my grave here, beside the Purest Branch.[8] This is the favour I ask.' So saying, he gave the man a gift of money.

That very evening, not long after sunset, word came that Nabíl of Qá'in had been taken ill. I went to his home at once. He was sitting up, and conversing. He was radiant, laughing and joking, but for no apparent reason the sweat was pouring off his face – it was rushing down. Except for this, he had nothing the matter with him. The perspiring went on and on; he weakened, lay in his bed, and toward morning, died.[9]

This is part of 'Abdu'l-Bahá's account of the life of Nabíl of Qá'in.

4

'Abdu'l-Bahá's Great Generosity

'Be ye daysprings of generosity, dawning-points of the mysteries of existence
. . .'[10]
                                     'Abdu'l-Bahá

When I was in Mázindarán[11] I was a wee bit of a child and enjoyed all the fun and play belonging to that age. In our town we had a man by the name of Áqá Rahím who was the overseer of our shepherds. One day he came to our house and asked my mother to let him take me to a country barbecue to be given by the shepherds. After some urging on his part, permission was granted, and I was glad of the chance to take part in an outdoor entertainment.

Áqá Rahím took me with him and soon we were out in the country. He led me through green valleys and beautiful pastures till we reached the foot of a lofty mountain. Here we had to walk through a narrow defile and then by a zig-zag road and with much difficulty slowly to ascend to the summit. When we arrived at the top I was surprised to find myself on a vast, verdant table-land which was no other than the pasture-land of our own cattle. I still feel the exhilarating breeze which greeted my cheeks on that clear day!

Exclusive of horses and cows there were about four thousand head of sheep and goats belonging to us, while a few thousand more were the property of other owners. But all were grazing peacefully on this broad plateau. It was a most charming, ideal pastoral scene and, from afar, I could see many shepherds and shepherdesses. We rode on a few minutes longer and then, under a spacious bower I was welcomed by some eighty or more shepherds who were clamouring to salute me. They were all dressed in their best clothes for this was a gala day. To me it was a noble and attractive sight.

On that morning about fifteen sheep had been killed and prepared in the cool-flowing spring near by; then the shepherds had stuck them on long iron rods to be roasted. Huge, spectacular campfires were burning and while the sheep were roasting the shepherds sang folk songs and danced their charming peasant dances. When noon came they all sat on the green grass and feasted, with extraordinary appetites, upon the well-seasoned, toothsome meat . . .

When evening drew nigh and the hour of our leave-taking approached all the shepherds gathered around us and in their farewell speeches hinted that they expected me to give them some gifts as is customary with the landlords in these parts. I asked Áqá Raḥím what it was all about and told him that as I was such a little child they should not expect me to make gifts and, moreover, I had brought nothing with me. Áqá Raḥím replied, 'This will not do. You are the master of all these shepherds and I do not like to think what they will say if you leave this place without giving them something.'

I was indeed in a dilemma but after thinking a moment the idea came to me to give each shepherd a few sheep from our own flocks. I communicated the idea to the overseer who was rather pleased with it; and it was announced in a solemn tone, and immediately acted upon. When at last we reached home, and my act of generosity was related to the Blessed Perfection, he laughed much over it and said, 'We must appoint a guardian to protect Áqá – master – from his own liberality; else, some day, he may give himself away.'[12]

'Abdu'l-Bahá's legendary generosity was manifest even in His early childhood.

5

This Black Servant Was Truly a Point of Light

'By My Life! The light of a good character surpasseth the light of the sun and the radiance thereof. Whoso attaineth unto it is accounted as a jewel among men.'[13]

Bahá'u'lláh

I had a servant who was black; his name was Isfandíyár. If a perfect man could be found in the world, that man was Isfandíyár. He was the essence of love, radiant with sanctity and perfection, luminous with light. Whenever I think of Isfandíyár, I am moved to tears, although he passed away fifty years ago. He was the faithful servant of Bahá'u'lláh and was entrusted with His secrets. For this reason the Sháh of Persia wanted him and inquired continually as to his whereabouts. Bahá'u'lláh was in prison, but the Sháh had commanded many persons to find Isfandíyár. Perhaps more than one hundred officers were appointed to search for him. If they had succeeded in catching him, they would not have killed him at once. They would have cut his flesh into pieces to force him to tell them the secrets of Bahá'u'lláh. But Isfandíyár with the utmost dignity used to walk in the streets and bazaars. One day he came to us. My mother, my sister and myself lived in a house near a corner. Because our enemies frequently injured us, we were intending to go to a place where they did not know us. I was a child at that time. At midnight Isfandíyár came in. My mother said, 'O Isfandíyár, there are a hundred policemen seeking for you. If they catch you, they will not kill you at once but will torture you with fire. They will cut off your fingers. They will cut off your ears. They will put out your eyes to force you to tell them the secrets of Bahá'u'lláh. Go away! Do not stay here.' He said, 'I cannot go because I owe money in the street and in the stores. How can I go?

'They will say that the servant of Bahá'u'lláh has bought

and consumed the goods and supplies of the storekeepers without paying for them. Unless I pay all these obligations, I cannot go. But if they take me, never mind. If they punish me, there is no harm in that. If they kill me, do not be grieved. But to go away is impossible. I must remain until I pay all I owe. Then I will go.' For one month Isfandíyár went about in the streets and bazaars. He had things to sell, and from his earnings he gradually paid his creditors. In fact, they were not his debts but the debts of the court, for all our properties had been confiscated. Everything we had was taken away from us. The only things that remained were our debts. Isfandíyár paid them in full; not a single penny remained unpaid. Then he came to us, said good-bye and went away. Afterward Bahá'u'lláh was released from prison. We went to Baghdád, and Isfandíyár came there. He wanted to stay in the same home. Bahá'u'lláh, the Blessed Perfection, said to him, 'When you fled away, there was a Persian minister who gave you shelter at a time when no one else could give you protection. Because he gave you shelter and protected you, you must be faithful to him. If he is satisfied to have you go, then come to us; but if he does not want you to go, do not leave him.' His master said, 'I do not want to be separated from Isfandíyár. Where can I find another like him, with such sincerity, such faithfulness, such character, such power? Where can I find one? O Isfandíyár! I am not willing that you should go, yet if you wish to go, let it be according to your own will.' But because the Blessed Perfection had said, 'You must be faithful,' Isfandíyár stayed with his master until he died. He was a point of light. Although his colour was black, yet his character was luminous; his mind was luminous; his face was luminous. Truly, he was a point of light.[14]

After relating this story, 'Abdu'l-Bahá said, 'Then it is evident that excellence does not depend upon colour. Character is the true criterion of humanity.'

6

An Extreme Case of Philanthropy

'Great is the blessedness awaiting the poor that endure patiently and conceal their sufferings, and well is it with the rich who bestow their riches on the needy and prefer them before themselves.'[15]
Bahá'u'lláh

Once Imám Ḥasan and Imám Ḥusayn both became ill. Their parents, His Holiness Imám 'Alí and His wife Fáṭimih,[16] vowed to fast when their children recovered. After some time the children became well and their parents fasted for three days. On the first day they baked four pieces of barley bread, one for each: 'Alí, Fáṭimih, Ḥasan and Ḥusayn. When the time arrived for them to break the fast, they heard someone at the door.

They asked after the identity of the visitor. It was a beggar, so they gave him all the bread and broke their own fast with water. On the second day the same thing happened. At the time of eating, someone knocked on the door and said that he was a slave. The four pieces of bread were given to him.

On the third day there was again a knock on the door and the man declared that he was homeless. As before, he received all the bread. Thus was revealed a verse[17] in the Qur'án directing the faithful to be generous towards the poor, the captive and the homeless and to give preference to these people over themselves.[18]

This story shows the importance of helping the poor and the needy.

7

An Extreme Case of Parsimony

'How many are the souls who with the utmost endeavour and effort, collect a handful of worldly goods and greatly rejoice in this act and yet in reality the Pen of the Most High hath decreed this wealth for others . . .'[19]

Bahá'u'lláh

Once upon a time there was a merchant in the city of Balsora.[20] His name was Reza. Although he was very wealthy he was the most close-fisted, narrow-hearted man that ever lived in his town. For avarice and penuriousness he had become a proverb among his countrymen. Through his stinginess he made his family suffer hunger and starvation.

In his office he had a clerk to whom he paid a very small salary. This clerk had a large family and though he practised the greatest economy he could not make both ends meet. Often he dreamed of a raise in his salary, but in vain. At last an idea flashed into his mind and gave him hope that surely there would be a raise soon. There was but one more week before New Year's day and the poor clerk thought that if he gave a present to his master he would undoubtedly reciprocate and increase his salary. Hence on that very day he went to the market, bought the head of a sheep, cooked it in his oven and carried it on a tray to his master. The week passed without any sign and finally, on New Year's day he called at the house of the merchant to wish him happiness. He was most hopeful, and anticipated a bright future.

When he entered the room, the merchant greeted him effusively. This made him more hopeful still.

'I thank you very heartily', the master said to his clerk, 'for the gift you sent to our house. It saved us a great deal of expense, I assure you. We have been feasting on it for the past week. The first day we ate the ears; the second day the eyes; the third day the skin of the head; the fourth day the tongue;

the fifth day the meat; the sixth day we cleaned the bones and on the seventh day we ate the brains.'

The clerk was so disgusted with this exhibition of stinginess that he left him, and left the town, and sought his fortune elsewhere.

After travelling for several years and acquiring experience as well as riches, he returned to his native city and opened a business of his own. One day as he was walking through the main street his attention was attracted by a most palatial residence. He peered through the gate and beheld a most beautiful garden. He finally inquired from one of the many servants lounging about whose house this was.

'Art thou a stranger?' they asked.

'Not exactly.'

'Well, how is it that thou dost not know that this is the residence of Kareem, the son of Reza?'

'Oh,' gasped the former clerk, 'what the father hoarded the son is spending!' – and disappeared through the crowd.[21]

Hoarding and miserliness are not commendable attributes.

8

The Horse Was Taken While Kafour Was Meditating

'The meditative faculty is akin to the mirror; if you put it before earthly objects it will reflect them.'[22]   'Abdu'l-Bahá

Once there was a man who had a . . . servant. His name was Kafour. Having decided to make a journey, he bought a horse, and took Kafour with him. After travelling all day, they reached a small ruined caravanserai, and realizing how tired they were they resolved to pass the night there, and refresh with sleep their weary bodies and continue their journey the next morning. As that locality was lately infested with robbers, they decided that the master should sleep until midnight, while Kafour kept guard over the horse. Then he (Kafour) would sleep in turn and the master would sit awake. After their supper the master slept, but after an hour he awoke and asked: 'Kafour, what are you doing?' He (Kafour) answered: 'I am meditating!' 'On what are you meditating?' 'I am meditating on the subject of – Why God has fashioned the edges of these thistles so sharp and cutting.' 'Very good!' the master chuckled to himself as he drew his head under the blanket, 'continue to meditate. That is a good subject.' Again he awoke half an hour before midnight and asked Kafour pleasantly: 'On what are you meditating now?' 'O Master! I am meditating as to who is going to carry on his back tomorrow morning the saddle and the bridle.'[23]

Carelessness and negligence cause deprivation.

9

Truth Saved the Life of the Man in the Basket

'Beautify your tongues, O people, with truthfulness, and adorn your souls with the ornament of honesty.'[24]   Bahá'u'lláh

King Solomon was a truthful man. One day a person sought his protection: he wanted Solomon to safeguard him against an enemy who was on his track.

Solomon happened to be carrying a large basket on that day. He told the man to get into the basket and the man did as he was told. Then Solomon put the basket on his head. Soon the man's enemy came to Solomon and asked him if he had seen the man.

Solomon said, 'Yes, he is in this basket on my head.'

The enemy said, 'Come on, man, this is not a time for joking.'

Solomon responded, 'The truth is what I have told you.'

The enemy did not believe him and resumed his chase.

Then Solomon told the man that his enemy was gone and that he could come out of the basket.

The man said, 'By the Almighty, O Solomon, I almost expired from fear. Why did you tell him that I was in the basket on your head?'

Solomon said, 'Deliverance is in truthfulness. Had I told him differently, he would not have believed me and would have probably killed both of us.'[25]

Truthfulness is a great virtue.

10

He Did Not Turn His Back on What Was Right

'O ye friends of God in His cities and His loved ones in His lands! This Wronged One enjoineth on you honesty and piety. Blessed the city that shineth by their light. Through them man is exalted, and the door of security is unlocked before the face of all creation.'[26]   Bahá'u'lláh

The distinguished 'Alí-'Askar was a merchant from Tabríz. He was much respected in Ádhirbáyján by all who knew him, and recognized for godliness and trustworthiness, for piety and strong faith. The people of Tabríz, one and all, acknowledged his excellence and praised his character and way of life, his qualities and talents. He was one of the earliest believers, and one of the most notable.

. . . the tyranny of the wicked brought him to an agonizing pass, and he was beset by new afflictions every day. Still, he did not slacken and was not dispirited; on the contrary, his faith, his certitude and self-sacrifice increased. Finally he could endure his homeland no more. Accompanied by his family, he arrived in Adrianople, and here, in financial straits, but content, he spent his days, with dignity, patience, acquiescence, and offering thanks.

Then he took a little merchandise with him from Adrianople, and left for the city of Jum'ih-Bázár, to earn his livelihood. What he had with him was trifling, but still, it was carried off by thieves. When the Persian Consul learned of this he presented a document to the Government, naming an enormous sum as the value of the stolen goods. By chance the thieves were caught and proved to be in possession of considerable funds. It was decided to investigate the case. The Consul called in Ḥájí 'Alí-'Askar and told him: 'These thieves are very rich. In my report to the Government, I wrote that the amount of the theft was great. Therefore you must attend the trial and testify conformably to what I wrote.'

The Ḥájí replied: 'Your Honour, Khán, the stolen goods amounted to very little. How can I report something that is not true? When they question me, I will give the facts exactly as they are. I consider this my duty, and only this.'

'Ḥájí,' said the Consul. 'We have a golden opportunity here; you and I can both profit by it. Don't let such a once-in-a-lifetime chance slip through your hands.'

The Ḥájí answered: 'Khán, how would I square it with God? Let me be. I shall tell the truth and nothing but the truth.'

The Consul was beside himself. He began to threaten and belabour 'Alí-'Askar. 'Do you want to make me out a liar?' he cried. 'Do you want to make me a laughing-stock? I will jail you; I will have you banished; there is no torment I will spare you. This very instant I will hand you over to the police, and I will tell them that you are an enemy of the state, and that you are to be manacled and taken to the Persian frontier.'

The Ḥájí only smiled. 'Jináb-i-<u>Kh</u>án,' he said. 'I have given up my life for the truth. I have nothing else. You are telling me to lie and bear false witness. Do with me as you please; I will not turn my back on what is right.'

When the Consul saw that there was no way to make 'Alí-'Askar testify to a falsehood, he said: 'It is better, then, for you to leave this place, so that I can inform the Government that the owner of the merchandise is no longer available and has gone away. Otherwise I shall be disgraced.'

The Ḥájí returned to Adrianople, and spoke not a word as to his stolen goods, but the matter became public knowledge and caused considerable surprise.[27]

A lesson in honesty and piety.

II

Truth Brought Success to This Mighty King

'Without truthfulness, progress and success in all of the worlds of God are impossible for a soul. When this holy attribute is established in man, all the divine qualities will also become realized.'[28]
'Abdu'l-Bahá

It is written that Nádir <u>Sh</u>áh[29] demanded that the governor of Baghdad should surrender the city to him. Since the governor was not militarily strong, he agreed that on a specified date he would surrender Baghdad to Iran.

While Nádir <u>Sh</u>áh was proceeding towards Baghdad, some 8,000 cavalrymen from Istanbul, under the leadership of 'U<u>th</u>mán Páshá, arrived in the city to give support to the governor.

Subsequently, the governor reneged on his promise and in the ensuing war Nádir <u>Sh</u>áh suffered a great defeat which forced him to take refuge in a mountain range. There he summoned his secretary and told him to write to headquarters: 'We have been beaten and many have been wounded, killed and captured. We are waiting here to receive ammunition and soldiers.'

However, the secretary wrote: 'By the grace of God, we scattered the forces of the Arab, killed thousands of the enemy, wounded many and taken prisoners of war. We demolished the enemy altogether. Now we are planning to attack other areas. We now await the arrival of troops and ammunition. That is all.'

Upon seeing this, Nádir Sháh became angry and told the secretary, 'Write exactly as I tell you. Write that our soldiers were fewer than theirs. Also, some 8,000 cavalrymen came to their aid. Therefore they refused to surrender the city as promised. They fought and defeated us. Many of our men were killed, wounded and captured. Now we are taking refuge in this mountain, waiting for winter to pass before beginning our second attack in the spring. We should now receive a bigger supply of ammunition, troops and military provisions than before. If God wishes, we will become victorious. That is all.'

By fate, it turned out this way. The following spring they attacked and were victorious.

Then Nádir Sháh said to his secretary, 'If I had covered up the truth and lied back then, no one would have believed our victory at this time.'[30]

'Abdu'l-Bahá told those in His presence that there is no need to lie – in the absence of news, it is better for reporters not to write anything at all.

12

An Unbelievably Truthful Spy

'Truthfulness is the foundation of all the virtues of the world of humanity.'[31]
'Abdu'l-Bahá

It is related that at the time of al-Amín and al-Ma'mún, the sons of Hárún ar-Rashíd,[32] there lived a truthful man who made a remarkable advance to a high position. Al-Ma'mún, with his huge army, started moving towards Baghdad.[33] Al-Amín sent a spy, whose name was 'Alí, to al-Ma'mún's camp.

When the two armies came within a league of one another, Ṭáhir, the commander of al-Ma'mún's army, emerged from his tent and began surveying the military manoeuvres. Suddenly, he noticed that a camel rider was moving at a great speed towards the camp. When he got close, Ṭáhir asked his name. The rider said his name was 'Alí.

Ṭáhir asked, 'What are you here for?'

'Alí answered, 'To spy.'

'Who has sent you?' Ṭáhir asked.

'Isau, the commander of al-Amín's army.'

Ṭáhir said, 'What do you want, exactly?'

'Alí told him, 'I want to do a thorough search here and then I want to return to al-Amín's camp and inform them of the situation.'

Ṭáhir took him to camp headquarters and assigned him a guide. He decreed that 'Alí could go anywhere and ask any questions he wanted. No one was supposed to hinder his work.

When 'Alí returned from his search and explorations, Ṭáhir asked him what he had done.

'Ali said, 'I did a thorough investigation, got to know your soldiers, weighed the quality of your commanders, inquired into your military expenditure, estimated your military equipment and learned of the mental attitude of your soldiers. I used all means of investigation and now, happily, I will return to my camp.'

Ṭáhir was astonished at the truthfulness and honesty of 'Alí. He showed him much hospitality and made him feel welcome. That night after dinner they made preparations for sleep. Ṭáhir noticed that 'Alí frequently raised his head from under the blanket and that he could not go to sleep.

Ṭáhir asked if anything was troubling him.

'Alí said, 'I am waiting for you to go to sleep so that I can run away.'

Ṭáhir said, 'All right, I'll sleep; you can go – with God's protection.' He pulled the blanket over his head and closed his eyes. 'Alí then escaped.

By chance, total victory in the battle went to al-Ma'mún; al-Amín was defeated.

After the conquest of Baghdad, Ṭáhir asked about 'Alí but 'Alí was in hiding. At last he was found and made the Minister of Finance. Ṭáhir said to him, 'If you had not been truthful, I would have killed you in the first instance. Since you were honest and steadfast in your opinion, you deserve to be the Minister of Finance.'[34]

This story demonstrates the value of honesty and truthfulness.

13

Lying Had Become His Second Nature

'When we find truth, constancy, fidelity, and love, we are happy; but if we meet with lying, faithlessness, and deceit, we are miserable.'[35]

'Abdu'l-Bahá

In Baghdad there was a man of Persian nobility who had fallen on hard times. He was even in need of his daily bread. This man, whose name was Zaynu'l-'Ábidín Khán, came to me one day, informed me of his condition and asked for my help. Muḥammad Khán, an Indian Rajah, was a friend of mine and I secured employment with him for Zaynu'l-'Ábidín Khán. The Rajah sent for him, favoured him highly and made him his own companion. He even allowed Zaynu'l-'Ábidín Khán to sit and have his meals at the same table with him. In addition, the Rajah offered him a monthly salary of twenty tumans.[36]

One day Zaynu'l-'Ábidín Khán came to me and said, 'Things could not be any better. But this Rajah hates lying and I have worked for many years in the Qájár[37] government and have become accustomed to lying. I am afraid that one day I might tell a lie, since I am accustomed to lying. As a consequence of this, I would be dismissed. Is it possible for you to talk to the Rajah about this issue?''

I said, 'How can I say such a thing to him?' I mentioned this in the presence of the Blessed Beauty, who smiled at the tale.

In the end, the Rajah dismissed Zaynu'l-'Ábidín Khán because he lied.[38]

'Abdu'l-Bahá explained that changing habits is difficult for some people.

14

He Lost His Son Over His Own Trustworthiness

'We should at all times manifest our truthfulness and sincerity, nay rather, we must be constant in our faithfulness and trustworthiness, and occupy ourselves in offering prayers for the good of all.'[39]   'Abdu'l-Bahá

Imru'l-Qays entrusted Samuel the Jew, who apparently lived in Syria, with a bag of money. The king of Jazira[40] learned of this, and to take the money, captured the lands surrounding Samuel's castle and besieged it.

Samuel said that this effort was of no avail and that he would not relinquish the money because it was a trust.

The fighting began and Samuel's son was killed. Nevertheless, Samuel resisted and did not give up custody of the trust until the arrival of the son of Imru'l-Qays, to whom he delivered the bag of money.[41]

'Abdu'l-Bahá was conversing with pilgrims about true civilization and the dissimilarities in ethics in different societies.

15

Penniless Qásim Bought 106 Bags of S͟hírází Tobacco

'Expect not that they who violate the ordinances of God will be trustworthy or sincere in the faith they profess. Avoid them, and preserve strict guard over thyself, lest their devices and mischief hurt thee.'[42]   Bahá'u'lláh

Qásim Nayrízí was exiled from Baghdad. He went to Mosul and from there he proceeded to 'Akká on foot. Afterwards, he went to Beirut with no money whatsoever. Visiting a tobacco store, he noticed that S͟hírází tobacco was being sold as Kás͟hí tobacco while the former was much more in demand. He purchased 106 bags of tobacco, and since he had no money, he went to Matí Farah, and said, 'I am a Bahá'í from 'Akká. I have made a purchase for which I am asking you to be my guarantor.' Matí Farah sent a cable to 'Akká and asked 'Abbúd if Qásim were telling the truth. 'Abbúd came to me and asked, 'Is Qásim Nayrízí a Bahá'í?' I said, 'Yes.' Thereupon, Matí Farah said that he would not guarantee Qásim but would pay cash. He paid in cash the price of 106 bags of tobacco. Qásim took all that tobacco to 'Akká, Haifa and Jaffa and sold it with much profit. Then he paid his debt to Matí Farah. After Qásim, there was a merchant by the name of 'Abdu'l-Ahad who borrowed heavily and returned none. He ruined that good name altogether. Were it not for that the Bahá'ís would now be in charge of all the trades in Syria.[43]

Information had been received that Bahá'í students had been accepted at the University of Beirut before they had paid for registration. 'Abdu'l-Bahá was

making a few remarks about establishing trust with people and treating them honourably.

16

He Was Made a Minister Despite His Reluctance

'Trustworthiness is the greatest portal leading unto the tranquillity and security of the people.'[44]

Bahá'u'lláh

It is related that at the time of 'Abdu'l-Malik ibn Marwán[45] there lived an honourable person who was also a brave commander. When the war broke out he was commissioned to go to the battlefield. Through his intelligence and foresight, he knew that one day his children might become needy. With this in mind, he went to a pious man and said, 'I am going to war and may never return. Therefore I am entrusting you with a sum of money, which is God's trust. If I come back, take a tenth of the amount and return the rest to me. But if I do not return, and my children become needy, take a tenth of the deposit for yourself and give the rest to them. Here is the trust: 10,000 tumans.' Then the renowned commander went to war and was subsequently killed.

Not too long after this, his children fell on hard times and became destitute. They were even in need of their daily bread.

One day the eldest son of the commander went to a religious man and informed him that they were so needy that they could not afford to write a letter to the caliph. The boy begged the man for assistance. With the help of this individual the boy wrote a letter and took it to the caliph but it did not bear any fruit.

The caliph said to him, 'If we dispense money like this, the country's treasury will soon be empty.' This caused the boy more pain and disappointment.

Later, the pious man became informed of the situation. He advised the boy of his father's trust and said, 'If you like, pay me the tenth, and if not, you don't have to pay.' The boy offered him twice as much instead but the pious man deducted only one-tenth and gave him the rest.

One day the caliph was listening to news of the war. He learned of the bravery of the military commander. He said, 'It is proper for us to extend some assistance to the commander's son who came to us for help.' Those who were listening informed the caliph that the boy had become rich and was no longer in need of assistance; then they related the story to the caliph.

He summoned both the pious man and the son of the commander. He asked them about the truth of the accounts he had heard. He then ordered that the key to the government's treasury be handed over to the pious man.

The man insisted that he had no qualifications for the job. He tried his best not to accept the position. The caliph did not agree with him, saying, 'Who is there better than you?'

Eventually the pious man became the government's treasurer.[46]

'Abdu'l-Bahá was talking to the pilgrims about the importance of piety and trustworthiness.

17

A Sinner Asked Forgiveness for Another Sinner

'The All-loving God created man to radiate the Divine light and to illuminate the world by his words, action and life.'[47]
                                                              'Abdu'l-Bahá

Fath̠-'Alí S̱h̲áh[48] had jailed some 200 Turkomans[49] he intended to kill. Mírzá Abu'l-Qásim, who was a Sufi, wrote to the king, bringing to his attention the fact that the people were innocent and did not deserve to be killed.

The king wrote back to him saying, 'If you take responsibility for my sins and intercede on my behalf on the Last Day (the Day of Judgement), I will free them.'

Mírzá wrote a marvellous reply. Indeed, he wrote with much sensitivity and tenderness. He prayed to God, saying, 'O God, a sinner is asking another sinner to act as his mediator. How can I intercede for him when I am aware of my own sins?' In closing he wrote, 'O God, the lives of innocent people are in danger and the king has conditioned their release upon my intercession. Because of this benevolent act, I intercede with Thee for him, while I confess my own sins. I hope the Almighty will forgive him for this good deed.'

He closed his letter by quoting some of the Mathnavi[50] poems.[51]

'Abdu'l-Bahá was commenting on historical events during the reign of Fath-'Alí Sháh.

18

The Wise and Grateful Ios, I

'Every one must show forth deeds that are pure and holy, for words are the property of all alike, whereas such deeds as these belong only to Our loved ones.'[52]
Bahá'u'lláh

Sulṭán Maḥmúd, a Ghaznavid king who ruled Iran from 998 to 1030, had a subject by the name of Ios (Ayaz) who, through a heroic action, had once rescued the King from great peril.

The memory of Ios haunted the King and his longing for the devoted shepherd grew so strong that at last he sent a messenger to summon the shepherd boy to the Royal Palace.

Unable to believe the good news, Ios came to the palace with eagerness and joy. Trembling with happiness he presented himself to the King.

The King was very pleased with Ios because Ios wanted nothing but to be near him. The King soon made him the guardian of his treasury, a position of great honour and responsibility.

But others who lived at the court of the King were jealous of the favour shown to Ios. They plotted together to try and find some fault with Ios so that they could destroy the King's trust in him. Day and night the courtiers kept watch on Ios and soon they found what they were seeking.

Each night, when everyone else was asleep, they would see Ios creep out of his room, stealthily wind his way through the corridors of the palace and climb the stairs to a small room at the top of one of the palace's many towers.

'Aha!' they whispered to themselves, 'he is robbing the King's treasure and storing it away secretly for himself.' And with glee, they hastened to take the news of their discovery to the King.

The King was angered and saddened at the news.

'I cannot believe this terrible thing you say of Ios,' he cried. 'Before I believe you I must see for myself if what you say is true.'

That night the King watched with the jealous courtiers. Sure enough, just as they had reported to him, Ios crept from his room and found his way to the small chamber in the tower. With sorrow the King followed and threw open the door of the little room with a mighty crash!

The room was completely bare and empty, except that on the wall hung the simple shepherd's coat which Ios had worn when he first met the King and the shepherd's crook he had used to tend his flock. Ios was sitting on the floor gazing at them.

'What is the meaning of this, Ios?' exclaimed the King, 'Why do you creep so quietly about my palace in the middle of the night, arousing my suspicions when I have raised you up and put my trust in you?'

'O my King,' replied Ios, 'when I first set my eyes on you I was a poor and ignorant shepherd boy. I have risen to this high position only through your bounty, favour and generosity. I wish never to forget what I was and from where I came so I may always remain humble and grateful to you. So, each night, I come here to think of what I was and what you, in your goodness and kindness, have made me.'

And the King marvelled at his fortune in having a servant as loyal and devoted as Ios.[53]

Man should adorn himself with praiseworthy qualities such as gratitude and humility.

19

The Wise and Grateful Ios, II

'Be generous in prosperity, and thankful in adversity.'[54]   Bahá'u'lláh

One day Sultán Maḥmúd cut open a melon and gave a piece to Ios, his much loved and trusted servant. Ios ate the piece and thanked the king with felicity. When the Sultán ate some of that same melon, he found it to be very bitter.

He asked Ios, 'How could you eat such a bitter melon and show no signs of vexation? Was it not bitter to you?'

'Yes it was bitter,' answered Ios, 'but I have received from your hand so many blessings and sweet things, it would be unjustifiable for me to complain about this one incident.'[55]

It is necessary to be thankful when beset by problems and difficulties. When surrounded by ease and abundance, everyone is happy and thankful.

20

The Wise and Grateful Ios, III

'Abandon not for that which perisheth an everlasting dominion, and cast not away celestial sovereignty for a worldly desire.'[56]
Bahá'u'lláh

Several years passed, and the King decided to go on a Royal Tour of his kingdom. Preparations started immediately and within a few days the magnificent procession was ready to leave. The ministers of the King's government, ambassadors and diplomats, courtiers and men of importance, soldiers and bandsmen, all splendid in their finery, set out to accompany the King. And, of course, the faithful Ios rode alongside his beloved master at the front of the throng.

Each evening the splendid party made camp and the wonderful imperial tent was erected for the King. This tent was the most beautiful and precious tent you have ever seen – woven from the finest silk, it was decorated with hundreds of jewels and precious stones, which so shone and sparkled in the lamp-light at night that the light of the moon and stars seemed to pale in comparison. Each night the King and his companions feasted and sang. Each morning, when the tent was struck, the jewels were collected and put in a box in the King's carriage.

Thus it was that the Royal Procession went on its way, the King looking contentedly at his peaceful and prosperous country, his followers happily riding and conversing during the day, and feasting and singing at night.

Then, one day, as the King and his retinue were making their way through some especially beautiful countryside, the King remembered that he had passed this way before. It had been on this very stretch of road, years ago, that he had first glanced upon the adoring face of his faithful Ios.

In gratitude for that meeting the King, seized of a sudden

impulse, took the box of jewels and cast them on the road.

As the procession went on its way the King looked back to see all his followers, all except Ios, forgetful of their duty, scrambling on the ground in great confusion trying to gather up the precious stones.

'Look at Ios,' they muttered to each other, 'see how proud he is, he even despises the King's jewels and makes no effort to pick them up.'

'How is it Ios,' the King asked him, 'that you do not join the others to gather up my jewels? Are they not precious? Do you despise the very things that were mine?'

'O my King,' replied Ios, 'never in my life have I despised the least thing that is yours. But to be near you and gaze on your face has always been more than sufficient for me. Why should I leave your side to scramble for what you have thrown away?'

And the loyal and steadfast Ios rode on by the side of his grateful master, his gaze never for a moment leaving the face of his beloved King.[57]

21

The Wise and Grateful Ios, IV

'Inasmuch as God is loving, why should we be unjust and unkind? As God manifests loyalty and mercy, why should we show forth enmity and hatred?'[58]
'Abdu'l-Bahá

The thing that the King prized above all his other many splendid possessions throughout the length and breadth of his kingdom was the Royal Garden. This garden was vast and very beautiful with trees and flowers, still lakes, clear-flowing streams and fountains. Within the bounds of the garden every living creature was safe and protected, for it was forbidden for anyone to kill anything in the garden.

Now the King so loved and trusted Ios that he made him the guardian and custodian of this Garden of Life and Beauty, the highest honour the King could bestow. Ios guarded his trust faithfully.

The King's son was the only one throughout the realm whom the King loved more than Ios. The young prince was the apple of his father's eye and in his father's sight he could do no wrong. Despite this, the prince was jealous of the trust and love that the King showed to Ios.

One day, as Ios was walking in the garden enjoying its beauty and ensuring that everything was as his royal master would wish, the young prince crept up stealthily behind Ios, and taking his bow, swiftly shot an arrow and as swiftly fled. The prince's arrow, true to his aim, struck down one of the royal swans. The blood flowed down the milky white breast into the clear water of the lake, and the swan swayed and drooped and died.

Ios stood horrified and grief-stricken, gazing first at the swan and then at the bow which had been thrown at his feet. As he stooped to pick up the bow one of the royal gardeners chanced by. Seeing Ios with the bow in his hand and the dead swan with its blood pinkly colouring the lake's pure water, he hastened straight away to tell the King what Ios had done.

The King summoned Ios to him.

'What have you done?' he demanded.

Ios bowed his head and remained silent.

'Speak!' the King commanded. 'Who killed the swan?'

But Ios, knowing the King's love for his son, would not answer.

Then, with a breaking heart, the King sternly exclaimed, 'Your silence condemns you. You have failed my trust. If you do not explain why you have done this terrible thing, I shall banish you forever from my presence.'

Silently, Ios lifted his eyes and took a long, last look at the face of his beloved King. Then he meekly bowed his head went out from the presence of the King and went alone into exile.

Time passed and the prince's conscience gave him no rest. He saw how his father, the King, grieved for Ios, and he observed that his father's love for him was in no way increased with the departure of the former shepherd boy. Then the news reached him that Ios was dying of a broken heart in his lonely hut far away.

Full of remorse he went to the King and threw himself at his father's feet.

'Forgive me, father, for the wrong I have done you and Ios,' he cried. And he confessed all that he had done.

The King in great grief sprang to his feet and cried out, 'Take me at once to Ios!'

In all haste the King sped to the lonely, far away hut and found Ios dying. Rushing to him, the King clasped him in his arms while the tears flowed freely from the royal eyes.

'O Ios, my beloved servant and friend, you must not leave me: you are my most loved and trusted servant, you have sacrificed your happiness and life for the sake of me and my son!'

Ios, resting in the arms of his dearly-loved master and gazing once again on the face of the one he loved so much, exclaimed, 'O my King, my master! Never have I sought anything but your pleasure. Now, having gazed once more upon your noble face, I die happy and content in Paradise!' Saying which, he passed peacefully away.[59]

This story is a lesson in true loyalty and self-sacrifice.

22

A Costly Dream

'O Son of Man! For everything there is a sign. The sign of love is fortitude under My decree and patience under My trials.'[60]

Bahá'u'lláh

There was a man who used to frequent rawḍih-khání[61] sessions and as soon as he would hear the eulogy about the martyrs in Karbalá and the cruel story of their deaths, he would take out a handkerchief and begin to cry loudly. He would say, 'I wish we were with you, O beloved Imám, so that we could have attained the greatest salvation.' He was always wishing to have been on the plain of Karbalá.

It so happened that one night he had a dream. In his dream he saw that Yazíd,[62] with his great army, was present in Karbalá. He also saw himself on the plain of Karbalá in the company of the Prince of Martyrs (Ḥusayn). Then he observed that 'Alí-Akbar[63] presented himself to the Imám, obtained permission for martyrdom, went to the battlefield and was martyred. Next came Qásim, who obtained permission, went to the field and lost his life. In this way several people were martyred, one by one.

Finally his turn arrived. The Imám ordered him to the battlefield. He asked, 'How can I go? I have no horse.'

His Holiness replied, 'Take my horse.'

He took the horse and mounted. Then he said, 'I have no sword.'

The Imám said, 'Take my sword.'

He took it. At this point he saw an excellent opportunity for escaping and he did just that. He chose fleeing over loyalty and firmness. In doing so, he took the Imám's horse and sword, leaving him without either. The following morning he narrated his dream to his relatives and friends.

The story reached the governor, who summoned him and said, 'I heard that you had a good dream. Tell me about it. It must be an interesting one.'

The man told him every detail of his dream. The governor asked, 'What would be the price of the Imám's horse?'
He said that it should have been at least 400 tumans. The
governor then asked him about the price of the sword.

He replied, 'About 300 tumans.'

After this, the governor ordered his men to take 700
tumans from the fellow before letting him go. Addressing
him, the governor said, 'You are an unjust person! Not only
did you refuse to help the Imám but you also took his
belongings and left him with neither horse nor sword. His
horse and sword were worth much more than 700 tumans
but you must pay the 700 tumans before you are released.'[64]

*This story was related with reference to Shaykh Ṣáliḥ who was very fearful
of the war which was then raging and who told 'Abdu'l-Bahá of his dreadful dreams about it.*

23

The Mullá Wanted His Finger Severed

*'The essence of faith is fewness of words and abundance of deeds; he whose
words exceed his deeds, know verily his death is better than his life.'*[65]

Bahá'u'lláh

Once a Mohammedan mullah [ákhúnd, Muslim priest, theologian, judge] thought that one of his fingers had become
impure, because he had touched an unclean article, and
consequently he thought that it must be cut off.[66] Passing by
the butcher's shop, he stopped and asked the butcher to cut
off his finger. 'I do not want it.' The butcher was astonished
and refused. The mullah explained his reason, and per-
sisted in his extraordinary demand. 'All right,' said the
butcher at last, 'put thy hand on this block of wood and I

will cut off thy finger.' Then taking his large cutting knife, he brought down, with apparent force, its blunt side on the hand of the mullah. No sooner had the mullah felt the harmless pain, than he pulled away his hand, while crying out and cursing the butcher for his merciless, cruel heart. 'O thou tyrant! What have I done to thee that thou wilt thus cut my hand?' he bemoaned. The butcher, realizing the utter weakness of the mullah, laughingly said, 'Go to; I did not harm thy hand. Thou coward, I just tested thee to see whether thou art made of heroic stuff.'[67]

'Abdu'l-Bahá's talk on that day can be summarized in His own words: 'Briefly, it is very easy to write and to speak upon these matters [high ideals], but it is hard to put them into action.'[68]

24

The Ruler Whose Deeds Did Not Match His Words

'Beware, O people of Bahá, lest ye walk in the ways of them whose words differ from their deeds.'[69]
Bahá'u'lláh

The Czar of Russia suggested the Hague Peace Conference and proposed a decrease in armament for all nations. In this Conference it was proved that Peace was beneficial to all countries, and that war destroyed trade, etc. The Czar's words were admirable though after the conference was over he himself was the first to declare war (against Japan).[70]

'Abdu'l-Bahá was speaking about the necessity for action. He said that high ideals need to be put into practice, not merely known or voiced.

25

The Mice Adopted a Great Plan Which Could Not Be Executed

'The central purpose of the divine religions is the establishment of peace and unity among mankind. Their reality is one; therefore, their accomplishment is one and universal . . .'[71]
'Abdu'l-Bahá

Once the rats and mice held an important conference the subject of which was how to make peace with the cat. After a long and heated discussion it was decided that the best thing to do would be to tie a bell around the neck of the cat so that the rats and mice would be warned of his movements and have time to get out of his way.

This seemed an excellent plan until the question arose as to who should undertake the dangerous job of belling the cat. None of the rats liked the idea and the mice thought they were altogether too weak. So the conference broke up in confusion.[72]

'Abdu'l-Bahá afterwards said that this story was reminiscent of the peace conferences which begin and end with words but have no tangible results.

26

He Lamented Over His Starving Dog

'A little earnestness and endeavour is encumbent upon you, so that the pages of the soul may be cleansed and purified from the rust of attachment to this ephemeral world.'[73]
'Abdu'l-Bahá

A poor Arab was sitting in a desert by the side of his dying dog, crying and lamenting over the imminent death of the animal. A wayfarer passing by asked him the reason for all his moaning and wailing.

The Arab said, 'This dog has been my constant companion and guard for a long time. Now he is dying of hunger and in this desolate place there is nothing that I can do to save him.'

The traveller, who was himself poor and without provision, felt sorry for the man and tried to say a few words of consolation, which was the only thing he could do. Therefore he began, 'It is not right to do so much weeping and lamenting over a dog.'

No sooner had he said this than the sound of the Arab's wailing became much louder, 'Alas! This is not a mere dog. He is my friend, a loyal and constant companion. He has performed great services and has rescued me from many dangerous situations.' He continued to recount the dog's numerous attributes and extolled him to the point that the wayfarer was truly moved with sorrow and sympathy and began crying over the plight of the man.

Some time passed and eventually the traveller raised himself from the ground to resume his journey. In the process of getting up he put his hand on the backpack of the Arab for support. As he did so, he heard a crunching sound. He asked the man what he had in his bag.

The Arab answered, 'It is dry bread, provision for my wandering.'

'Why don't you give some of it to your dog?' asked the wayfarer.

This question displeased the Arab, who stared at the traveller and said, 'I do not like him enough to give him my own bread.'[74]

A story about insincerity and selfishness.

27

Chocolate-Coated Quinine

'Ye are even as the star, which riseth ere the dawn, and which, though it seem radiant and luminous, leadeth the wayfarers of My city astray into the paths of perdition.'[75]
Bahá'u'lláh

Once there was a young man who left his country and resided in Egypt for six years in order to study the science of physiognomy.[76] During this long period he studied hard and suffered much in the foreign land. Finally he reaped the benefit of all the hardships he had endured. He succeeded in all his theoretical and practical examinations and obtained a degree in physiognomy. He was quite pleased with this hard-earned success and joyfully began his journey home, riding a mule.

During the long journey back to his home town, he had many hours to practise his acquired skills in the field of physiognomy. Whenever he would see a person, he would carefully study his features and deduce something about him. One day on the road he saw a man some distance away. He saw in that man all the signs of stinginess, envy, greed and meanness. He said to himself, 'O God! In Thee we seek refuge from Thy wrath. Such sinister and ill-omened features I have never known or seen before. I wish I could become acquainted with this person, so that I could test my own observations and knowledge.'

He was submerged in such thoughts when the strange man, with a happy and smiling face, approached him and said, 'O Shaykh, if I may ask your eminence, where are you coming from and where are you going?'

The Shaykh said that he had started his trip in Egypt, was proceeding towards his own home town and planned to stay in a certain village for the night.

The stranger said politely, 'Sir, that village is far. It is getting late in the day and my house is very close. I would be most happy if you would honour my house with your presence.'

The Shaykh noticed that his own deductions were in complete contrast with the man's words and deeds. He therefore became doubtful of his knowledge, and in order to further test himself, he accepted the stranger's invitation and followed him to his house.

Happily and willingly the stranger extended to the Shaykh a cordial reception and much hospitality. He brought his guest refreshments of all kinds, as well as a water pipe, and repeatedly urged him to partake of the food. At the stranger's insistence the Shaykh helped himself to some of the refreshments and tried to enjoy this unexpected hospitality. However, every time his gracious host would speak to him with kindness, he would sigh and think to himself that all his time and effort had been wasted and that his studies had been in vain.

When dinner time arrived the Shaykh saw that the table, which was loaded with a great variety of food, was ready for him. Again, he regretted his misjudging a very good and generous man for a mean and stingy one. After dinner he went to bed feeling quite depressed and dejected.

Early in the morning the Shaykh wanted to leave but his host would not consent. With many kind and friendly words he persuaded the Shaykh to stay for lunch and made all the necessary arrangements for his ease and comfort. All in all, owing to the stranger's insistence, the Shaykh remained as a guest in that house for three days and nights.

Finally the Shaykh succeeded in convincing his host that he needed to be on his way. When it became clear that the Shaykh was going to leave, the stranger groomed and readied the mule and very respectfully helped his guest to mount. Then he held the harness of the mule firmly in one hand and with the other delivered a paper bag to the Shaykh. Assuming that the bag contained some provisions for his journey, the <u>Shaykh</u> asked the stranger about its contents. The man answered that it contained a statement of his account, which he must pay before leaving.

The <u>Shaykh</u> asked, 'What account?'

At this point the stranger emerged from his sheath of pretence and the veil of hypocrisy was removed from his face. He wrinkled his eyebrows, made a grim face and said, 'Did you think that all those things you consumed were free?'

The <u>Shaykh</u>, who was rudely jarred to his senses, opened the bag, looked at the bill and saw that whatever he had eaten or looked at had been charged to him at a price a hundred times higher than the market price. Knowing that he had nothing close to the amount he was supposed to pay, he dismounted his mule and gave it and the saddle bag and all that it contained to the stranger.

Then, happy and thankful to God that his six years of study and effort had not been in vain, he started the rest of his journey back home on foot.[77]

In 'Akká there was a doctor who was spiteful towards the Bahá'ís. He would treat sick Bahá'ís and render excellent services but would then charge them enormously high fees. 'Abdu'l-Bahá related this story one day after He had paid in full the doctor's excessive charges.

28

The Poor Man Was Too Attached to His Donkey

'I have sought reunion with Thee, O my Master, yet have I failed to attain thereto save through the knowledge of detachment from aught save Thee. I have yearned for Thy love, but failed to find it except in renouncing everything other than Thyself.'[78]

The Báb

There were two friends, one a rich man who had detachment and the other a poor yet worldly man. At the suggestion of the latter, the two suddenly decided to embark on a pilgrimage to the holy land, leaving everything behind. Realizing that his rich friend was indeed leaving all his belongings behind and that he had no intention of returning, the poor man said, 'Now that we are really leaving, wait here for a little while so that I can go back and bring my donkey.'

The rich man said, 'Then you are not the right person for this journey. You cannot dispense with one donkey. At your suggestion, I have started on this journey, leaving everything behind. I never entertained the thought of returning, despite my great wealth. You have nothing but a donkey and for that you want to return!'[79]

'Abdu'l-Bahá told the friends in Paris that detachment is freedom from attachment to worldly things and has nothing to do with being rich or poor.

29

His Poverty and Weakness Were Accepted

'O Son of Passion! Cleanse thyself from the defilement of riches and in perfect peace advance into the realm of poverty; that from the well-spring of detachment thou mayest quaff the wine of immortal life.'[80]　　Bahá'u'lláh

Ustád Ismá'il walked to 'Akká to see Bahá'u'lláh. However, when he arrived the gate was barred. He stood behind the second moat to catch a glimpse of his Lord in the prison window but his eyesight failed him and he turned back in grief.

He made his home in a cave outside the city. He put a few inexpensive rings, thimbles and pins on a tray and walked the streets from morn till noon. He earned 20 to 30 copper pieces a day, at best 40. Then he would go back to his cave-home to eat his meagre meals and to praise and magnify the Name of his Lord. He was always contented and thankful.[81]

'Abdu'l-Bahá said that Bahá'u'lláh was heard to express His satisfaction with Ustád Ismá'il.

30

The Poor Wolf Lost the Deer and His Own Head Too

'That is, a religious individual must disregard his personal desires and seek in whatever way he can wholeheartedly to serve the public interest; and it is impossible for a human being to turn aside from his own selfish advantages and sacrifice his own good for the good of the community except through true religious faith.'[82]

'Abdu'l-Bahá

A lion, a wolf, and fox went hunting. They captured a wild ass, a gazelle, and a hare. The lion said to the wolf, 'Divide the spoil.' The wolf said, 'That is easy; the ass for yourself, the gazelle for me, and the hare for the fox.' The lion bit off the wolf's head saying, 'You are not a good divider.' Then turning to the fox, he said, 'You divide.' The fox said, 'The ass, the gazelle, and the hare are yours.' The lion looking at him, said, 'Because you have accounted yourself as nothing, you may take all the prey.'[83]

Self-abnegation is a praiseworthy attitude.

31

Abú-<u>Dh</u>arr Thought He Was Content

'The source of all good is trust in God, submission unto His command, and contentment with His holy will and pleasure.'[84]

Bahá'u'lláh

39

Once Salmán invited Abú-<u>Dh</u>arr[85] for lunch but he brought only two loaves of bread. Abú-<u>Dh</u>arr said, 'O Salmán, don't you have something else to go with this bread?'

Salmán felt ashamed. He had a cooking pot which he pawned to get money, bought some yogurt and offered it to Abú-<u>Dh</u>arr.

After he finished eating, Abú-<u>Dh</u>arr said, 'Praised be God, some food was consumed with contentment and frugality.'

Salman said, 'By God, this was not contentment. If you had been content and happy with the bread, my only cooking pot would not have been bartered away.'[86]

ʿAbduʾl-Bahá was telling His listeners that they should be content with small things, must teach the Cause and try to render service at His threshold.

32

His Shirt Interfered with His Rest

'Disencumber yourselves of all attachment to this world and the vanities thereof. Beware that ye approach them not, inasmuch as they prompt you to walk after your own lusts and covetous desires, and hinder you from entering the straight and glorious Path.'[87]   Baháʾuʾlláh

Most of the time the early Baháʾís of Iran travelled on foot. Wherever they became tired, there they would sleep or rest under the shade of a tree.

Once, one of the Baháʾís became acquainted with a prince who wanted to give him a present. With much insistence the prince made him accept a shirt. In the course of his next journey, when the fellow became tired, he used the shirt as his head-rest and lay down to sleep under a tree. Yet he could not go to sleep because of his doubts and anxieties; repeatedly he imagined that a thief was about to steal his newly acquired shirt. At last he got up and threw the shirt away, saying, 'As long as this shirt is with me and I am attached to it, I will not feel comfortable or relaxed.'[88]

'Abdu'l-Bahá was talking about detachment and freedom from the cares of this world.

33

A Wood-Chopper Must Eventually Stop Chopping

'I have made death a messenger of joy to thee. Wherefore dost thou grieve? I made the light to shed on thee its splendour. Why dost thou veil thyself there-from?'[89]
                                                                    Bahá'u'lláh

When the Baha'is were staying in Adrianople there was a Baktashi who lived close by them. Professionally he was a wood-chopper, socially he was a wit. Once, he became severely ill and was on the eve of departure from this world. Becoming acquainted with this fact, [I] called on him. He was lying on a low, uncomfortable cot, and his old wife was sitting beside it with the marks of solicitude and care on her wrinkled face, 'Thou art going to get well very soon. This sickness shall pass away and thou wilt be strong. Oh, my beloved! I am praying to Allah for thy speedy recovery. May Allah hear my prayers!' The sick man, as though pulling himself out of a heavy drowsiness, half-opened his eyes and said: 'What can I do even if I get well? I am tired of the world and want to leave it, my dear. Oh! I am so weary, so weary.' And he closed his eyes. The wife, with much agitation declared: 'Oh no, no! May Allah never bring that black day! My darling! Thou wilt gain back thy health, my beloved. Together we will go into the garden and there eat all kinds of fruits. Hand in hand we will walk through the woods and listen to the songs of the birds. Yes, yes, I will nurse thee back to health, oh thou, the apple of my eye!'

The sick man, without opening his eyes, and seemingly with much struggle, answered her back: 'Oh my wife, be silent! Nothing shall happen if I get well only this: I have to chop ten or twenty or thirty more loads of wood. That's all. Have I not cut enough already? Oh, please let me die.'[90]

In this world we are all wood-choppers.

34

He Was Martyred Because He Wanted to Be

'Lord! Have mercy upon me, lift me up unto Thyself and make me to drink from the Chalice of Martyrdom, for the wide world with all its vastness can no longer contain me.'[91]

'Abdu'l-Bahá

One of the much respected people who suffered martyrdom at the fort of Shaykh Ṭabarsí was a man named Murshid. His Eminence Murshid, who had accepted the Bábí Faith in Tehran, used to have good relationships with important people. He was among the defenders of the fort who trusted the oath that the enemy inscribed and sealed on the Qur'án and therefore surrendered to them. They took him to Mihdí Qulí Mírzá.[92]

Sulaymán Khán, who was one of the leaders in the army, knew Murshid. As soon as his eyes fell upon Murshid, he was greatly surprised and shouted, 'O Murshid! What are you doing here?'

Murshid answered, 'Yes, accidents of the world!'

Sulaymán Khán said, 'You must thank God for sending me here in order to save your life. Otherwise they would have killed you instantly.'

With a moving and earnest voice, Murshid responded, 'O Sulaymán Khán! If you want to reward me for the sake of our old friendship, I beg you not to intervene on my behalf.

Otherwise, I would be deprived of the bounty of martyrdom, would fall behind my friends and would become a captive of this world again. I have seen and experienced all that this world has to offer. No longer do I have any attachment to or affection for it. Now I just want to go and visit the next world.'

After this, he was martyred.[93]

People of great faith and true understanding are eager to take their flight to the next world.

35

This Youth Danced to the Scene of His Martyrdom

'O Son of Man! By My beauty! To tinge thy hair with thy blood is greater in My sight than the creation of the universe and the light of both worlds.'[94]

Bahá'u'lláh

One day, whilst at Káẓimayn, through which He passed on his first journey to Karbila and Baghdád, Jamál-i-Mubárak was appealed to by a young man, 'Abdu'l-Vahháb, who was much attracted to Him, saying:

'One request, my Lord. My father and my mother have come to spend their latter days, and to die, in this holy place. They are very fanatical! I pray that they may be given grace to drink of the Chalice of Life.'

Bahá'u'lláh answered: 'Persuade your father to come to me.'

To his father the youth went, saying:

'O my father, there is here an honourable person from Tihrán, who, although wearing a *kuláh*, not a turban, is a surging sea of divine knowledge; he has a shining countenance, and a radiance of joy and happiness is with him, surely we should go to see him.'

His father, as soon as he came into the presence of Jamál-i-Mubárak, exclaimed:

'Oh! Lord, we have heard One calling us to faith, therefore we believe. Forgive us our sins.'[95]

Immediately he, having understood and believed, began to teach publicly, and became a famous Bábí.

'Abdu'l-Vahháb (the son) implored to be allowed to accompany Bahá'u'lláh; he was, however, directed to remain with his parents, whose love for him was very great. 'Abdu'l-Vahháb continued to ask his father's permission to join Bahá'u'lláh. To this at length the father agreed, and the young man made his way to Tihrán, where he was unable to find his beloved Lord.

He, meanwhile, proceeded to teach the people openly in the street, ignoring all personal risk.

Now took place the deplorable incident of the insane youth shooting at the Sháh. Mírzá 'Abdu'l-Vahháb was instantly seized and thrown into the horrible prison, where very soon Bahá'u'lláh Himself arrived, having been arrested at His village, Níyávarán, whence He had been made to walk barefoot, with heavy chains on His neck, and fetters on His limbs; in this condition, without His *kuláh*, did the friends see their Beloved.

Mírzá 'Abdu'l-Vahháb spent a few days in that dungeon in great joy and happiness, for was he not in the presence of Him, Whom he recognized as his Lord?

Each day would the executioner come and call out certain names.

'Abdu'l-Vahháb's turn came. He arose and danced in the prison, knowing that his hour of martyrdom had come. He kissed the beloved hand, and gave himself over into the hands of the executioner and his assistant torturers.

When the news reached his father, he bowed his head and thanked God that his sacrifice had been accepted at the Divine Threshold.[96]

Juliet Thompson heard 'Abdu'l-Bahá's dramatic exposition of the story of this martyred youth, at the end of which He told her, 'See! the effect that the death of a martyr has in the world. It has changed my condition.'

36

A Timid Man Became a Dauntless Martyr

'Supremely lofty will be thy station, if thou remainest steadfast in the Cause of thy Lord.'[97]
Bahá'u'lláh

Mirza Ghorban Ali [Mírzá Qurbán-'Alí], who was one of the Seven Martyrs [of Ṭihrán], a man of great piety and learning, was a strong Babi, but he was very fearful and timid. He was so fearful of being known as a Babi that when he met the friends in the streets he would not look at them. He shunned their association. Yet the enemies found him out somehow, and brought him into the prison house. As he was well known among the military class for his wisdom and devotion, two of these influential officers went to Mirza Tagi Khan [Mírzá Taqí Khán][98] the Prime Minister, and interceded for him. When the Prime Minister found out that such important men were interceding for him, he became very lenient and told them to bring [Mírzá Qurbán-'Alí] to him so that he might recant. This Prime Minister was such a domineering and blood-thirsty man that the army was in constant fear of him, so that when he was reviewing the army if he just turned his eyes upon one of the soldiers he would tremble and shake with fear. Finally these two officers took Mirza Ghorban Ali to the Prime Minister, and they were so happy in the thought that he would be released before long. When he came before the Prime Minister, the Prime Minister looked at him and said: 'These friends of yours have interceded for you. Are you ready to repudiate Ali Mohammed ['Alí-Muḥammad, the

45

Báb]?' Mirza Ghorban Ali, looking around, saw the executioner about fifteen feet from him, standing, and then he
turned to the Minister and asked, 'Whom shall I repudiate,
Ali or Mohammed?' (Mohammed being the Prophet and
Ali the son-in-law, they are considered the Holy Ones in the
Mohammedan world. The name of the Bab is composed of
these two.) The Prime Minister became so angry that he
ordered the executioners to take him away and kill him and
he left the presence of the Prime Minister with serene face
and a heavenly smile on his countenance.[99]

*Before telling this story 'Abdu'l-Bahá said: 'At the time of trials, wonderful
confirmations descend upon man, regenerating him and making him a new
creation.'*[100]

37

The Firm Believer Prayed to Die with the Báb

*'O Son of Man! Ponder and reflect. Is it thy wish to die upon thy bed, or to
shed thy life-blood on the dust, a martyr in My path, and so become the manifestation of My command and the revealer of My light in the highest
paradise? Judge thou aright, O servant!'*[101]   Bahá'u'lláh

Among the disciples of the Báb . . . were two: His amanuensis and a firm believer. On the eve of the Báb's
martyrdom the firm believer prayed: 'Oh let me die with
You!' The amanuensis said: 'What shall I do?'
   '"What shall I do?" . . . What do you want me to do?'
The disciple died with the Báb, his head on the breast of
the Báb, and their bodies were mingled in death. The other
one died in prison anyway, but think of the difference in
their stations!'[102]

Just before telling this story, 'Abdu'l-Bahá said, 'Do you remember the rich young man who wanted to live near Christ, and when he learned what it cost to live near Him – that it meant to give away all his possessions and take up a cross and follow Christ – then he fled away!'

38

The Emperor Who Disliked His Own Image

'Abandon not the everlasting beauty for a beauty that must die, and set not your affections on this mortal world of dust.'[103] Bahá'u'lláh

There was an elderly emperor who used to look at himself in the mirror and express sentiments of sorrow and grief. He would say, 'What a healthy and fine body I had but how shrunken it has now become! What a beautiful face I had but how ugly it has now become! I had such an elegant stature but it has now become so bent!' He would recount his youthful conditions one by one and express his grief and indignation over their decline.[104]

'Abdu'l-Bahá told a Bahá'í woman from Philadelphia that she should try to be happy all the time. He told her that spirituality is the cause of everlasting happiness while material happiness is subject to shift and change.

39

Even a King Cannot Claim to be Truly Happy

'No matter how far the material world advances, it cannot establish the happiness of mankind. Only when material and spiritual civilization are linked and coordinated will happiness be assured.'[105] 'Abdu'l-Bahá

His Holiness Solomon said, 'When I was a child I used to think that happiness was riding a horse or going on an outing. When I became a juvenile I went on many excursions and did a lot of horseback riding.

'Soon I realized that they did not give real pleasure. Then I told myself that happiness must be in ruling and in being a powerful king. After I became a king I understood that this too did not bring a true and lasting happiness. It was the same with everything else in the world. When I obtained whatever seemed desirable and interesting to me, I found that very thing to be unattractive. Finally I realized that real happiness is in the love of God.'[106]

In His talk 'Abdu'l-Bahá conveyed the message that happiness in this world does not endure very long but spiritual happiness and tranquillity in the love of God last forever.

40

He Never Stayed in the Same Palace Twice in a Year

'Set before thine eyes God's unerring Balance and, as one standing in His Presence, weigh in that Balance thine actions every day, every moment of thy life. Bring thyself to account ere thou art summoned to a reckoning . . .'[107]

Bahá'u'lláh

It is written that in the Diyarbakr[108] lived Ibn-i-Mashtoot, who was one of the first successful kings of Islam. All means of happiness were at his disposal, from every side. During his reign no disturbing events caused him worry and his entire domain was at complete peace and security. A few times he fought against the Crusaders and every time he prevailed. For many years he ruled and encountered no problems whatsoever. He was also much favoured by the caliph,[109] so much so that the caliph dismissed his own minister and told him to become the minister of Ibn-i-Mashtoot.

This king had 360 palaces and in each one he kept a wife who was from a renowned family. He would spend one day and one night in each palace and during the entire year he would not stay in the same palace twice. The lady whose turn it was to receive the king would arrange for dancing and music and would do her best to make available to the king all means of pleasure and happiness.

Shortly before his death the king cried and said, 'All this is in vain! Why did I busy myself with these childish affairs which all end in manifest loss? Would that I had been a farmer and had spent my time in useful and meritorious activities.'[110]

Position, fame and wealth in this world do not bring about an everlasting happiness.

41

The Sultan Who Wept and Wept

'To the eternal I call thee, yet thou dost seek that which perisheth. What hath made thee turn away from Our desire and seek thine own?'[111]   Bahá'u'lláh

It is related that Saboktakeen [Sebuktegin],[112] one of the renowned ancient kings of Persia, lived in the utmost grandeur and splendour. His palace was like unto the delectable paradise, and his table was provided with royal bounty and his life was like unto a stream of milk and honey. His treasuries were full and his riches unlimited. He was in the utmost joy and happiness. Suddenly he was attacked with a malady and was burning away like unto a candle and with Jeremiads of disappointments he was singing the most mournful tunes. His treasuries and all his precious jewels were on display before his eyes, and his accumulated wealth was arrayed in dazzling fashion. Then

he invited his ministers, courtiers and statesmen to be present in the throne room on a certain hour, and asked his
immense army to be engaged in manoeuvres of victory and
triumph in the military square in front of the palace. While
sitting on his throne, he looked regretfully now on this
scene, now on another, and again on all this matchless array
of grandeur and magnificence and wept most bitterly, crying aloud, 'O! Why must I be deprived of this imperial
sovereignty and these royal prerogatives? Why should I not
enjoy this life? Why bid farewell to all these things? How
can I leave them behind and hasten empty-handed from
this world to another world?' He wept and wept till he drew
his last breath.[113]

*In connection with this story, 'Abdu'l-Bahá said, 'At the end, grief and regrets
are the allotment of the people of wealth, except those who spend their riches
on philanthropic causes.'*[114]

42

The Dying King Wished He Had Been a Poor Man

*'Man is, in reality, a spiritual being, and only when he lives in the spirit is
he truly happy.'*[115]
                                                                'Abdu'l-Bahá

On his deathbed, a king wished he had been a poor man.
He would often say, 'Would that I had been a poor man so
that I would not have perpetrated tyranny and at this part-
ing time would not have so many regrets.'
    A poor man heard this and said, 'Thank God that at the
end of their earthly lives some kings wish to have been poor.
However, we never wish at such a time to have been
kings.'[116]

Before telling this story, 'Abdu'l-Bahá said, 'A patient poor man is better than a thankful rich one. But a thankful poor man is better than a patient one. The best, however, is a generous rich man.'

43

The Three Men Created a Puzzling Spectacle

'O Companion of My Throne! Hear no evil, and see no evil, abase not thy-self, neither sigh and weep.'[117]
Bahá'u'lláh

A man once, as he was walking, saw a wonderful sight. In a certain place there were three men. The first of these was blind, but he could see things that were very distant. The second was deaf to all near sounds, but he could hear things that were very far off. The third was naked, but he held in his hands very carefully, a long hem of a garment. The man asked a teacher the meaning of this strange sight. The interpretation of it was this: These three men represent humanity. The first, who could only see things that were very distant, but was blind to all that was near him, means that people can generally see very clearly the faults and shortcomings of other natures, and of those who are far from them; but their own faults are too near them to be per-ceived. The second man was able to hear of the deaths of others; but his own death was too near him to be heard. The third, who was quite bare, shows that in this state man comes into this world; and in this state it is quite certain he must leave it – and though he knows this very well, yet he spends his whole time in carefully preserving the hem of a garment from being soiled.[118]

'Abdu'l-Bahá was commenting on a verse from the Bible, 'Neither do I con-demn thee: go, and sin no more'.[119]

44

The Just Persian Monarch

'The foundation of the Kingdom of God is laid upon justice, fairness, mercy, sympathy and kindness to every soul.'[120]　　　　　'Abdu'l-Bahá

That fair-minded monarch [Anúshírván[121]] came to power at a time when the once solidly established throne of Persia was about to crumble away. With his Divine gift of intellect, he laid the foundations of justice, uprooting oppression and tyranny and gathering the scattered peoples of Persia under the wings of his dominion. Thanks to the restoring influence of his continual care, Persia, which had lain withered and desolate, was quickened into life and rapidly changed into the fairest of all flourishing nations. He rebuilt and reinforced the disorganized powers of the state, and the renown of his righteousness and justice echoed across the seven climes, until the peoples rose up out of their degradation and misery to the heights of felicity and honour. Although he was a Magian, Muḥammad, that Centre of creation and Sun of prophethood, said of him: 'I was born in the time of a just king', and rejoiced at having come into the world during his reign.[122]

'Abdu'l-Bahá makes the point that greatness is achieved by virtue of admirable qualities and not by reaching out to conquer the earth and spilling the blood of its people.

45

The Sultan and the Woman Who Knew the Qur'án

'Observe, O King, with thine inmost heart and with thy whole being, the precepts of God, and walk not in the paths of the oppressor.'[123]　　　Bahá'u'lláh

When Sultan Sanjar[124] entered Nís̲h̲apúr,[125] he ordered all its inhabitants to vacate their homes in order to make room for the lodging and comfort of his soldiers. A woman went to him and said, 'I take care of the orphans, I know the Qur'án by heart and I have four houses. Take three of them and leave at least one for me.'

The Sultan replied, 'You claim to know the Qur'án by heart. Have you heard, "The kings, when they enter a township, despoil it"?'[126]

She said, 'I have read even further, to where it says, "Their tyranny brings misery to its people."'[127]

The Sultan cried out and expelled his soldiers from the place.[128]

'Abdu'l-Bahá was talking to the pilgrims about some events in the history of Persia.

46

All the Guns Were Fired but Not a Single Coyote Was Hit

'Thank God thou didst become a soldier of life; subdued the domain of hearts with the arms of the love of God and the sword of concord and peace . . .'[129]

'Abdu'l-Bahá

During the reign of 'Abdu'l-Ḥamíd when a group of soldiers volunteered to fight against the Russians each soldier was given a gun and 200 bullets. There was a man by the name of S̲h̲ákir Pás̲h̲á who related the following.

'The clerics were in our regiment. After we left Istanbul, whenever we saw a crow, a vulture or a fox all the guns would be suddenly fired. They would say, "Fire, fire." Our repeated warning that the ammunition was to be used against the enemy was of no use. By the time we reached the border they had used all their bullets. Incidentally, they did not kill even a single fox, coyote or crow. On the border we had to climb a hill and establish an encampment. The clerics said that they would stay right where they were. Meanwhile, the Russians took position on that hill. They were firing at us continuously. We suggested then that we should go to the other side and set up a more advantageous position. The clerics maintained that their position was quite suitable and that they would sit right where they were. At any rate, the Russian army approached from another side and captured them. After returning from the war, it was decreed that this ragtag group should be thrown out by the rifle butts. Despite all their begging and pleading, we ordered them, "Be gone and get lost!"[130]

'Abdu'l-Bahá was talking about the defensive manoeuvres of the Ottoman government against the British battleships.

47

This Poor Man Had Some Good Questions for the King

'If the rulers and kings of the earth, the symbols of the power of God, exalted be His glory, arise and resolve to dedicate themselves to whatever will promote the highest interests of the whole of humanity, the reign of justice will assuredly be established amongst the children of men, and the effulgence of its light will envelop the whole earth.'[131]   Bahá'u'lláh

A Persian king was one night in his palace, living in the greatest luxury and comfort. Through excessive joy and gladness he addressed a certain man, saying: 'Of all my life this is the happiest moment. Praise be to God, from every point prosperity appears and fortune smiles! My treasury is full and the army is well taken care of. My palaces are many; my land unlimited; my family is well off; my honour and sovereignty are great. What more could I want!'

The poor man at the gate of his palace spoke out, saying: 'O kind king! Assuming that you are from every point of view so happy, free from every worry and sadness – do you not worry for us? You say that on your own account you have no worries – but do you never worry about the poor in your land? Is it becoming or meet that you should be so well off and we in such dire want and need? In view of our needs and troubles how can you rest in your palace, how can you even say that you are free from worries and sorrows? As a ruler you must not be so egoistic as to think of yourself alone but you must think of those who are your subjects. When we are comfortable then you will be comfortable; when we are in misery how can you, as a king, be in happiness?'[132]

Before relating this story, 'Abdu'l-Bahá stated, 'The good pleasure of God consists in the welfare of all the individual members of mankind.'

48

Burning a Minister's Tent Restored Order

'There is no glory for him that committeth disorder on the earth after it hath been made so good. Fear God, O people, and be not of them that act unjustly.'[133]
                                                                    Bahá'u'lláh

After some disturbances in a military camp, Ḥajjáj[134] the tyrant was put in charge. The first rule he issued was that all of the tents should be raised at the same time and lowered at the same time.

The next time camp was broken all the tents except one came down at the same time. That one tent belonged to a government minister.

Immediately, Ḥajjáj ordered the tent to be burned down. This action served as a lesson to the others and caused the order of the camp to be established.[135]

ʿAbduʾl-Bahá was talking to the Iranian minister plenipotentiary and a group of distinguished people from the East and West about some historical events in Islam. By telling this story, He was making the point that exceptions create chaos.

49

The Cool-Headed Emperor

'Say: Sow not, O people, the seeds of dissension amongst men, and contend not with your neighbour. Be patient under all conditions, and place your whole trust and confidence in God. Aid ye your Lord with the sword of wisdom and utterance.'[136]   Baháʾuʾlláh

It is written that once Bonaparte[137] was busy writing. Suddenly, a cannon ball from the enemy's camp landed near his tent and exploded. This caused some dirt to be scattered over his writing.

This incident did not disturb Bonaparte at all. He paused a little and said, 'I am grateful that the enemy helped me in my work. In order to dry the ink quickly, I would have put some soil on this letter myself.[138] The enemy helped me to finish my task more quickly so that now I can begin my assault.'

He then issued the order to attack. The trumpets were sounded and, by chance, he was victorious.[139]

Some of the friends were talking about news of the war. They were apprehensive about the bombing raids. ʿAbduʾl-Bahá told them that they should not be disturbed, that they should be confident and remain composed.

50

The King Wanted to Hear the Sermon by Telephone

'Take heed lest pride deter you from recognizing the Source of Revelation, lest the things of this world shut you out as by a veil from Him Who is the Creator of heaven.'[140]   Bahá'u'lláh

Every year, on the occasion of the arrival of the New Year, the Pope would deliver a sermon in the church. One year he invited the Italian king to attend this ceremony.

The king did not accept the invitation. He said, 'A telephone line must be installed between the church and my palace so that I can listen to the Pope's sermon from here.'[141]

This story was related by 'Abdu'l-Bahá when He was talking about His three-day stopover in Naples in the course of His journey to the West.

51

Abraham Rebuked His Idol-Worshipping Guest

'So intense must be the spirit of love and loving kindness, that the stranger may find himself a friend, the enemy a true brother, no difference whatsoever existing between them. For universality is of God and all limitations earthly.'[142]   'Abdu'l-Bahá

It is related that an aged and decrepit man became the guest of his holiness Abraham. He exercised toward his guest the utmost hospitality and courtesy. When dinner was served, his holiness Abraham uttered the name of God, and then started eating. On the other hand, the guest uttered the name of an idol and began to eat. His holiness was grieved, arose in wrath and rebuked his guest most severely.

But even as he did so, God's revelation descended upon him. 'O Abraham! For a hundred years this man has been an idol-worshipper and I have been patient with him; I have nurtured him; I have protected him. I have taken good care of him; I have trained him, I have showered on him many bounties and I have been kind and loving to him; but thou wert not able to endure his society one night! And I, a hundred years!' His holiness Abraham was deeply touched by this address and begged his aged guest to pardon him.[143]

This story is about the universality of love and acceptance.

52

Everyone Became Rich and Moses Became Helpless

'For the community needs financier, farmer, merchant and labourer just as an army must be composed of commander, officers and privates. All cannot be commanders; all cannot be officers or privates.'[144]   'Abdu'l-Bahá

According to a Muslim parable, Moses once prayed to God saying, 'O God, why aren't all people rich?' He begged God to make all the people wealthy and everybody became rich.

The very first night after this the house of Moses needed some repair. He tried to fetch a mason. The mason refused to come; he informed Moses that he was rich and was therefore in no need of work. The carpenter and the labourer likewise refused. Moses became helpless.

Then He heard a voice from above saying, 'O Moses, it is the requirement of divine wisdom that there be ranks and degrees, otherwise the order of the world will break down.'[145]

'Abdu'l-Bahá was telling those in His company that a society cannot function if all its members are absolutely equal.

53

Elijah Trained People on God's Mountain

'Ye are the shepherds of mankind; liberate ye your flocks from the wolves of evil passions and desires, and adorn them with the ornament of the fear of God.'[146]   Bahá'u'lláh

His Holiness Elijah dwelt in a cave below this spot. At that time all the children of Israel were opposed to the religion of God. They were engaged in their own passions and pursuits. Only their name indicated that they were the people of His Holiness Moses. If His Holiness Moses had come among them at that time he would not have recognized them. He would have said: 'I do not consider them as my own, for they have entirely forsaken the religion of God. They are deprived of the law of God. There is no light at all remaining in them . . .'

Then His Holiness Elijah educated certain souls in this cave. He educated pure and sincere souls as they ought to be and sent them among the children of Israel. They began to teach and call the children of Israel back to God. They called them back again to the law of God. [At one time] His Holiness Elijah gathered all their chief men together and brought them to the top of this mountain [Carmel]. There were three hundred and sixty of these chief men. But however much he taught and counselled them he obtained no result. He tried to guide them, but it was no use. For several years he worked to educate them. At the end no result was apparent. He realized that they would corrupt other souls. Then he had these three hundred and sixty men put to death. Then the rest of the children of Israel returned to their original spiritual morals and behaviour. Then they regained their spiritual life. The everlasting glory again became apparent. They overcame the neighbouring tribes. They rebuilt the Holy Temple. The laws of God were put into effect.

Then, when His Holiness Elijah had finished his work he left . . . and went away. He retired. They thought he had ascended to Heaven. But no, having accomplished his work, he retired. He had no attachment to the world. When his object was accomplished he retired from the world. When he realized that his work was done he devoted himself to his own development.[147]

'Abdu'l-Bahá was on Mount Carmel, near the Tomb of the Báb. He spoke of the beauty of the mountain and its spiritual atmosphere.

54

The Zoroastrian High Priest Was Flogged

'And of all men, the most accomplished, the most distinguished and the most excellent are the Manifestations of the Sun of Truth. Nay, all else besides these Manifestations, live by the operation of their Will, and move and have their being through the outpourings of their grace.'[148]
                                                                    Bahá'u'lláh

When the Muslims conquered Persia, the chief of the Zoroastrian high priests went to drink wine. According to Muslim law, wine is forbidden, and he who drinks it must be punished by eighty-one strokes of the whip. Therefore, the Muslims arrested the high priest and whipped him. At that time the Arabs were considered very low and degraded by the Persians, scarcely to be accounted as human beings. As Muḥammad was an Arab, the Persians looked upon Him with disdain; but when the high priest saw evidences of a power in Muḥammad which controlled these despised people, he cried out, 'O thou Arabian Muḥammad, what hast thou done? What hast thou done which has made thy people arrest the chief high priest of the Zoroastrians for committing something unlawful in thy religion?'[149]

'Abdu'l-Bahá's talk was about the great power of the word of Bahá'u'lláh and other Manifestations of God.

55

Buddha's Disciples Passed the Test

'We must gird ourselves for service, kindle love's flame, and burn away in its heat.'[150]

'Abdu'l-Bahá

Buddha had disciples and he wished to send them out into the world to teach, so he asked them questions to see if they were prepared as he would have them be. 'When you go to the East and to the West,' said the Buddha, 'and the people shut their doors to you and refuse to speak to you, what will you do?' The disciples answered and said: 'We shall be very thankful that they do us no harm.' 'Then if they do you harm and mock, what will you do?' 'We shall be very thankful that they do not give us worse treatment.' 'If they throw you into prison?' 'We shall still be grateful that they do not kill us.' 'What if they were to kill you?' the Master asked for the last time. 'Still,' answered the disciples, 'we will be thankful, for they cause us to be martyrs. What more glorious fate is there than this, to die for the glory of God?' And the Buddha said: 'Well done!'[151]

In response to a question concerning Buddhism, 'Abdu'l-Bahá said, 'The real teaching of Buddha is the same as the teaching of Jesus Christ. The teachings of all the Prophets are the same in character.'[152]

56

Christ Declared Himself the Richest Man on Earth

'The essence of understanding is to testify to one's poverty, and submit to the Will of the Lord, the Sovereign, the Gracious, the All-Powerful.'[153]

Bahá'u'lláh

Jesus was a poor man. One night when He was out in the fields, the rain began to fall. He had no place to go for shelter so He lifted His eyes toward heaven, saying, 'O Father! For the birds of the air Thou hast created nests, for the sheep a fold, for the animals dens, for the fish places of refuge, but for Me Thou hast provided no shelter. There is no place where I may lay My head. My bed consists of the cold ground; My lamps at night are the stars, and My food is the grass of the field. Yet who upon earth is richer than I? For the greatest blessing Thou hast not given to the rich and mighty but unto Me, for Thou hast given Me the poor. To me Thou hast granted this blessing. They are Mine. Therefore am I the richest man on earth.'[154]

'Abdu'l-Bahá told those at the Bowery Mission in New York City that the poor are very dear to God.

57

A Great Lesson

'O ye Cohorts of God! Beware lest ye offend the feelings of anyone, or sadden the heart of any person, or move the tongue in reproach of and finding fault with anybody . . .'[155]   'Abdu'l-Bahá

According to a proverb, His Holiness Christ, may my life be a sacrifice to Him, was passing with His disciples along a road.

Seeing a dead dog, one of the disciples said, 'So foul-smelling is this corpse.'

Another said, 'So loathsome is its face.'

The next one said, 'How offensive and disgusting a spectacle it is.'

Each one of them had something to add to the list.

Then His Holiness Christ said, 'Yes but see how white and beautiful are his teeth.'[156]

'Abdu'l-Bahá teaches us, 'One must see in every human being only that which is worthy of praise.'[157]

58

Christ Unearthed a Hidden Treasure

'This is the changeless Faith of God, eternal in the past, eternal in the future. Let him that seeketh, attain it . . .'[158]   Bahá'u'lláh

It is related that one day Jesus entered a village where the authorities had decreed that its inhabitants should not entertain any strangers in their homes. This was because of the many robberies that were taking place in the village at that time. Jesus stopped at the door of an old woman.

When the woman saw His dignity and gentleness, she was ashamed and could not refuse Him shelter. She therefore extended to Him her hospitality and showed Him much respect. From His bearing and demeanour she soon realized that she was entertaining more than an ordinary mortal. She approached Christ, kissed His hand and said, 'I have only one son and nobody else in this world. He used to be a good worker and we were living in happiness and comfort. Recently, however, he has become disturbed, irritable and sad. He has filled our house with much sorrow and anxiety. He goes to work during the day but when he returns home at night he is agitated and temperamental and cannot sleep. He never answers any of the questions put to him.' Jesus told the woman to send the boy to Him.

That night the boy returned home. His mother went to him and said, 'My son, our guest tonight is a great person. If anything is troubling you, share it with Him.' The son went to Jesus and sat down.

Jesus said, 'Tell me, my son, what is the cause of your worries?'

He replied, 'Nothing.'

Christ said, 'You are not telling the truth – something is greatly troubling you. Tell me about it. You can trust me and confide in me. I do not divulge the secrets of people. Be assured that I will keep your secret.'

The boy complained, 'I am afflicted with a pain that has no remedy.'

Jesus offered, 'Tell me, I will cure it for you.'

The boy repeated his assertion that his sickness had no cure but Jesus assured him that He could solve any problem.

Then the boy admitted, 'I am ashamed and it is impolite to talk about it.'

Jesus explained, 'I am your Father; I will forgive you.'

So the boy began, 'Near this village is a city in which the king lives. I have fallen in love with his daughter. I am only a thorn-picker; what else can I say?'

Jesus told him, 'Rest assured that I will make your wish come true.' In brief, Jesus made all the necessary arrangements and the boy married the girl.

That night when the young man entered the bridal chamber, which was a highly decorated room, a thought suddenly sprang to his mind. 'Jesus made such an extraordinary arrangement for me. Why didn't He do it for Himself?

If He could do it for me, surely He could have done it for Himself. Despite His great transcendent power, He roams in the wilderness eating grass, sleeping on the ground, sitting in the darkness of the night and leading a life of poverty.'

No sooner had these thoughts come to the young man than he turned to his bride and said, 'Wait right here, I have important business to attend to. I will go now but will return as soon as I can.' With this, he left the room and went out searching for Christ. Eventually he found Him and addressed Him, saying, 'O my Lord, you were not just towards me. You treated me unfairly.'

'How can that be? Did I not help you attain your heart's desire?' replied Jesus.

The boy responded, 'Yes, yes, but you obtained for me that which you do not want for yourself. Surely you must possess something far greater and more important than what you gave me. If what you gave me was worthy of possession, you would have certainly chosen it for yourself. It is obvious, therefore, that you must possess something of greater value than the things you bestowed upon me. Accordingly, you have dealt with me unjustly.'

Jesus said to him, 'You are indeed speaking the truth but are you capable and worthy of receiving this greater gift?' The boy expressed his hope of being worthy of such a gift. 'Can you forget all these worldly things and leave them behind?'

'Yes, my Lord,' was his eager reply.

Then Jesus said, 'With me, you will find the path to the Almighty, which is greater than all these worldly things. Now, if you can, follow me.'

The young man then followed Christ, who went straight to His disciples and said, 'I had a treasure which was hidden in a village near by. I have just unearthed it and I now give it to you. Here is my treasure.'[159]

'Abdu'l-Bahá was speaking about the greatness of Jesus Christ.

59

Christ's Body Was Crucified but His Reality is Eternal

'The Christ Kingdom was everlasting, eternal in the heaven of the divine Will.'[160]   'Abdu'l-Bahá

. . . the disciples were agitated when they saw the body of Jesus crucified. Then Mary Magdalen came to them and said: 'Why are you agitated?' 'Because,' they replied, 'Jesus has been crucified.' 'Oh,' she said, 'that was the body of Jesus, but the Reality of Jesus is living and eternal. *It* is not subject to corruption.'[161]

'Abdu'l-Bahá was answering a question regarding the personality of the Manifestation of God.

60

The Disciples Held a Council on the Mount

'The Great Being saith: The heaven of divine wisdom is illumined with the two luminaries of consultation and compassion. Take ye counsel together in all matters, inasmuch as consultation is the lamp of guidance which leadeth the way, and is the bestower of understanding.'[162]   Bahá'u'lláh

The most memorable instance of spiritual consultation was the meeting of the disciples of Jesus Christ upon the mount after His ascension. They said, 'Jesus Christ has been crucified, and we have no longer association and intercourse with Him in His physical body; therefore, we must be loyal and faithful to Him, we must be grateful and appreciate Him, for He has raised us from the dead, He made us wise, He has given us eternal life. What shall we do to be faithful to Him?' And so they held council. One of them said, 'We must detach ourselves from the chains and fetters of the world; otherwise, we cannot be faithful.' The others replied, 'That is so.' Another said, 'Either we must be married and faithful to our wives and children or serve our Lord free from these ties. We cannot be occupied with the care and provision for families and at the same time herald the Kingdom in the wilderness. Therefore, let those who are unmarried remain so, and those who have married provide means of sustenance and comfort for their families and then go forth to spread the message of glad tidings.' There were no dissenting voices; all agreed, saying, 'That is right.' A third disciple said, 'To perform worthy deeds in the Kingdom we must be further self-sacrificing. From now on we should forego ease and bodily comfort, accept every difficulty, forget self and teach the Cause of God.' This found acceptance and approval by all the others. Finally a fourth disciple said, 'There is still another aspect to our faith and unity. For Jesus' sake we shall be beaten, imprisoned and exiled. They may kill us. Let us receive this lesson now. Let us realize and resolve that though we are beaten, banished, cursed, spat upon and led forth to be killed, we shall accept all this joyfully, loving those who hate and wound us.' All the disciples replied, 'Surely we will – it is agreed; this is right.' Then they descended from the summit of the mountain, and each went forth in a different direction upon his divine mission.[163]

'Abdu'l-Bahá was explaining the nature of true consultation.

61

The Christians Intervened on Behalf of the Jews

'Mary Magdalene was a villager of lowly type, yet that selfsame Mary was

transformed and became the means through which the confirmation of God descended upon the disciples.'[164]   'Abdu'l-Bahá

One of the services of Mary Magdalene after the crucifixion of Christ was accomplished through her audience with the Emperor of Rome.[165] This happened after both Pilate and Herod realized that the Jews had instigated the Messiah's martyrdom through slander and that Jesus was innocent. They therefore harassed the Jews.

Through some means Mary saw the Emperor and when he asked her about her purpose, she said, 'I am sent here by the Christians, who want to intercede on behalf of the Jews. They request that the Jews be left in peace, even though they were the instigators of Christ's death. He would not be happy with this vengeance.'

The Emperor was very happy with, and quite impressed by the words of Mary, and he ordered a stop to all the hostile acts against the Jews.[166]

'Abdu'l-Bahá's talk centred on the greatness of Mary Magdalene and her services to the cause of Christianity.

62

The Bishop with a Problem Meets a Clever Boy

'All that is mentioned of the Manifestations and Dawning-places of God signifies the divine reflection, and not a descent into the conditions of existence.'[167]
                              'Abdu'l-Bahá

It is said that once John of Chrysostom[168] was walking along the seashore and thinking over the question of the trinity. He was wondering how three could become one and one could become three. He wanted to reconcile this theological issue with reason and logic.

Soon his attention was attracted to a boy sitting on the shore scooping sea water into a cup. Approaching him, he asked the boy what he was doing.

'I want to put all of the sea water into this cup,' was the answer.

John said, 'How foolish you are in trying to do the impossible. How could you possibly put all of that sea water into this little container?'

The boy replied, 'Your work is stranger than mine, for you are labouring to bring within the grasp of human intellect the concept of the trinity.'[169]

In His response to a question about the relationship between God and His Messengers, 'Abdu'l-Bahá likened them to mirrors in which is reflected the sun of divinity.

63

The Emperor Becomes a Christian Out of Necessity

'Although nearly twenty centuries have elapsed since Christ appeared with divine splendour, yet the Jews are still awaiting the coming of the Messiah and regard themselves as true and Christ as false.'[170]   'Abdu'l-Bahá

When Christ appeared, all the powers tried to uproot His Cause. The governors as well as the people. Twelve times they were massacred. Most of the Christians were killed. Notwithstanding this, it continued to spread. Many people were killed, many houses were destroyed, people were imprisoned, but in spite of all this it spread.

In France, Louis strove much. He killed many. He deported many from his country. Then he began to realize that he had failed to uproot the Cause of Christ. At last he began to realize that he should uplift it. Then he sum-

moned his ministers and consulted them. He said: 'I see
that our future is very bad. The more I try to extinguish
this Light the brighter it becomes. I think this Flag of
Christ will bring down our flag. Therefore before our flag
comes down, let us yield to it.' They laughed at this. They
were not thinking of the future. They were the embodi-
ment of prejudice . . . He quitted them. Then he sent for
a Christian who was influential and trustworthy. He said:
'I have repented. I want to be under the Banner of Christ.
I want to become a Christian. What shall I do?'

He replied: 'Empty one of these temples, throw out all
the idols, remodel it, raise up a bell and proclaim that on
Sunday you will go to church for the proclamation of the
Cause of Christ.'

On Sunday, with his robes and all his ministers and all his
family, he drove in state, with dignity and glory, to the
church. He entered and took off his hat. He asked a
Christian to pray. All of them prayed. Then he came out
and proclaimed that his religion was the religion of Christ.[171]

The religion of God progresses despite all opposition.

64

By Keeping His Promise Ḥanzala Awakened the King

'Religion confers upon man eternal life and guides his footsteps in the world
of morality.'[172]
'Abdu'l-Bahá

The Arabian chronicles tell how, at a time prior to the
advent of Muḥammad, Nu'mán son of Mundhir the
Lakhmite – an Arab king in the Days of Ignorance, whose
seat of government was the city of Ḥírih – had one day
returned so often to his wine-cup that his mind clouded

over and his reason deserted him. In this drunken and insensible condition he gave orders that his two boon companions, his close and much-loved friends, K͟hálid son of Mudallil and 'Amr son of Mas'úd-Kaldih, should be put to death. When he wakened after his carousal, he inquired for the two friends and was given the grievous news. He was sick at heart, and because of his intense love and longing for them, he built two splendid monuments over their two graves and he named these the Smeared-With-Blood.

Then he set apart two days out of the year, in memory of the two companions, and he called one of them the Day of Evil and one the Day of Grace. Every year on these two appointed days he would issue forth with pomp and circumstance and sit between the monuments. If, on the Day of Evil, his eye fell on any soul, that person would be put to death; but on the Day of Grace, whoever passed would be overwhelmed with gifts and benefits. Such was his rule, sealed with a mighty oath and always rigidly observed.

One day the king mounted his horse, that was called Maḥmúd, and rode out into the plains to hunt. Suddenly in the distance he caught sight of a wild donkey. Nu'mán urged on his horse to overtake it, and galloped away at such speed that he was cut off from his retinue. As night approached, the king was hopelessly lost. Then he made out a tent, far off in the desert, and he turned his horse and headed toward it. When he reached the entrance of the tent he asked, 'Will you receive a guest?' The owner (who was Ḥanzala, son of Abí-G͟hafráy-i-Ṭá'í) replied, 'Yea.' He came forward and helped Nu'mán to dismount. Then he went to his wife and told her, 'There are clear signs of greatness in the bearing of this person. Do your best to show him hospitality, and make ready a feast.' His wife said, 'We have a ewe. Sacrifice it. And I have saved a little flour against such a day.' Ḥanzala first milked the ewe and carried a bowl of milk to Nu'mán, and then he slaughtered her and prepared a meal; and what with his friendliness and

71

loving-kindness, Nu'mán spent that night in peace and comfort. When dawn came, Nu'mán made ready to leave, and he said to Ḥanzala: 'You have shown me the utmost generosity, receiving and feasting me. I am Nu'mán, son of Munḏhir, and I shall eagerly await your arrival at my court.'

Time passed, and famine fell on the land of Ṭayy. Ḥanzala was in dire need and for this reason he sought out the king. By a strange coincidence he arrived on the Day of Evil. Nu'mán was greatly troubled in spirit. He began to reproach his friend, saying, 'Why did you come to your friend on this day of all days? For this is the Day of Evil, that is, the Day of Wrath and the Day of Distress. This day, should my eyes alight on Qábús, my only son, he should not escape with his life. Now ask me whatever favour you will.'

Ḥanzala said: 'I knew nothing of your Day of Evil. As for the gifts of this life, they are meant for the living, and since I at this hour must drink of death, what can all the world's storehouses avail me now?'

Nu'mán said, 'There is no help for this.'

Ḥanzala told him: 'Respite me, then, that I may go back to my wife and make my testament. Next year I shall return, on the Day of Evil.'

Nu'mán then asked for a guarantor, so that, if Ḥanzala should break his word, this guarantor would be put to death instead. Ḥanzala, helpless and bewildered, looked about him. Then his gaze fell on one of Nu'mán's retinue, Sharík, son of 'Amr, son of Qays of Shaybán, and to him he recited these lines: 'O my partner, O son of 'Amr! Is there any escape from death? O brother of every afflicted one! O brother of him who is brotherless! O brother of Nu'mán, in thee today is a surety for the Shaykh. Where is Shaybán the noble – may the All-Merciful favour him!' But Sharík only answered, 'O my brother, a man cannot gamble with his life.' At this the victim could not tell where to turn. Then a man named Qarád, son of Adja' the Kalbite stood up and offered himself as a surety, agreeing that, should he fail on the next Day of Wrath to deliver up the victim, the king might do with him, Qarád, as he wished. Nu'mán then bestowed five hundred camels on Ḥanzala, and sent him home.

In the following year on the Day of Evil, as soon as the true dawn broke in the sky, Nu'mán as was his custom set out with pomp and pageantry and made for the two mausoleums called the Smeared-With-Blood. He brought Qarád along, to wreak his kingly wrath upon him. The pillars of the state then loosed their tongues and begged for mercy, imploring the king to respite Qarád until sundown, for they hoped that Ḥanzala might yet return; but the king's purpose was to spare the life of Ḥanzala, and to requite his hospitality by putting Qarád to death in his place. As the sun began to set, they stripped off the garments of Qarád, and made ready to sever his head. At that moment a rider appeared in the distance, galloping at top speed. Nu'mán said to the swordsman, 'Why delayest thou?' The ministers said, 'Perchance it is Ḥanzala who comes.' And when the rider drew near, they saw it was none other.

Nu'mán was sorely displeased. He said, 'Thou fool! Thou didst slip away once from the clutching fingers of death; must thou provoke him now a second time?'

And Ḥanzala answered, 'Sweet in my mouth and pleasant on my tongue is the poison of death, at the thought of redeeming my pledge.'

Nu'mán asked, 'What could be the reason for this trustworthiness, this regard for thine obligation and this concern for thine oath?' And Ḥanzala answered, 'It is my faith in the one God and in the Books that have come down from heaven.' Nu'mán asked, 'What Faith dost thou profess?' And Ḥanzala said, 'It was the holy breaths of Jesus that brought me to life. I follow the straight pathway of Christ, the Spirit of God.' Nu'mán said, 'Let me inhale these sweet aromas of the Spirit.'

So it was that Ḥanzala drew out the white hand of guidance from the bosom of the love of God, and illumined the sight and the insight of the beholders with the Gospel light. After he had in bell-like accents recited some of the divine verses out of the Evangel, Nu'mán and all his ministers sickened of their idols and their idol-worship and were confirmed in the Faith of God. And they said, 'Alas, a thousand times alas, that up to now we were careless of this infinite mercy and veiled away therefrom, and were bereft of this rain from the clouds of the grace of God.' Then straightway the king tore down the two monuments called the Smeared-With-Blood, and he repented of his tyranny and established justice in the land.[173]

Before relating this story 'Abdu'l-Bahá wrote, '. . . the Faith of God must be propagated through human perfections, through qualities that are excellent and pleasing, and spiritual behaviour.'[174]

65

The King of Egypt Was Astute in His Forecast

'From the pulpit-top there ascendeth today the words of praise which, in utter lowliness, glorify His blessed name; and from the heights of minarets there resoundeth the call that summoneth the concourse of His people to adore Him.'[175]

Bahá'u'lláh

Once a trading caravan from Mecca was passing through Syrian lands. The Egyptian king ordered that the leader of the expedition be brought to him. Accordingly, Abú Sufyán,[176] who was in charge of the caravan, was taken to him. The king told him that he had heard rumours about the Ḥijáz[177] and he wanted to know the truth about what was going on there.

Abú Sufyán said, 'Nothing important – an illiterate orphan by the name of Muḥammad, in collaboration with some highwaymen and other low people, is earning his livelihood by stealing and raiding caravans. Once they raided us and took everything. We had to assemble a caravan of a large number of men and many provisions. Owing to this preparation, we have become immune to their raids.'

The king told him that he was not interested in that sort of thing and that he had some questions to which he wanted correct answers. He continued, 'I will do some investigation of my own and if I discover that your answers have been false, I will punish you next year when you cross this land again. Be careful to answer all my questions truthfully.' Abú Sufyán promised to tell the truth. Then the king asked, 'Was this Muḥammad crazy before He made His claim?'

Abú Sufyán answered, 'No, He was not mad.'

'Was He a prince?'

'No,' replied Abú Sufyán.

The king inquired, 'Did His worldly affairs improve or did He become more comfortable after His claim?'

Abú Sufyán said, 'No, on the contrary, He became helpless and a wanderer.'

The king paused a bit and asked again, 'Did He slacken in His claim or slow down in His work after He became the target of persecution?'

'No, He grew more insistent and intense.'

And again the king asked, 'Is He gaining or losing ground?'

Abú Sufyán explained, 'More and more people are gathering around Him and they agree with His ideas.'

'Are His followers from among the rich, the dignitaries, or from among the poor and the homeless?'

'The learned and the rich are not with Him at all.'

The king said, 'Do the people who accept Him become respected, comfortable and wealthy?'

'Not at all, they all become humiliated and are forced to flee their homes,' answered Abú Sufyán.

The king thought a short while and then asked his last

question. 'Do these men, who become despised and home-less because of their belief in Muḥammad, grow weaker in their faith or stronger?' 'Abú Sufyán told him, 'Not weaker. On the contrary, they become firmer and stronger.'

Then the king commanded, 'O Abú Sufyán, it is your duty to submit to Him as soon as you can.'

Abú Sufyán said, 'No, sir. He is not worthy of this posi-tion at all. He will soon fade away.'

The king replied, 'You poor fellow, you don't seem to understand. If you have answered my questions truthfully, not only you and the Arabian tribes but also the Emperor of Rome and I must soon submit to Him. Otherwise He will force us to yield.'[178]

'Abdu'l-Bahá was speaking on the progress of the Cause of God and the fact that no earthly power can stop its growth. He gave historical examples of the futility of the opposition of the wayward to the religions of the past.

66

Since 'We' Encompassed Abú-Bakr, He Became the Caliph

'The departure of Muḥammad, the Beloved of God, from the city of His birth was the cause of exaltation of God's Holy Word, and the banishment of the Sacred Beauty led to the diffusion of the light of His divine Revelation throughout all regions.'[179]   'Abdu'l-Bahá

After Muḥammad migrated to Medina and God's care and protection was extended to Him, He said to Abú-Bakr,[180] who was in His company, 'Do not be sad, God is indeed with us.' This very sentence was the cause of Abú-Bakr's ascension to the post of caliph. Some people put forward the argument that Abú-Bakr was included in the words 'with us'. So from this utterance they drew conclusions.[181]

The topic of discussion was the importance of 'Abdu'l-Bahá's travels in the West.

67

Muḥammad's Fantastic Promises Were Fulfilled

'Aye! The promise of God is a truth. Let not this present life deceive you concerning God.'[182]   Muḥammad

In the process of digging a trench (in preparation for the War of the Trench), the Muslims encountered a huge rock which could not be moved. Muḥammad became annoyed, hit the rock with his staff and said, 'Behold, the enemies are defeated.' Again He hit the rock and said, 'Behold, the Emperors' domain (Roman empire) is conquered.' A third time He hit the rock and said, 'Behold, the Khusraws' dominion (Persian empire) is conquered.'

The companions were surprised to hear these words and the Hypocrites[183] began scorning the Prophet. One of them said to the other, 'How can this man promise us the treasuries of Rome and Persia when we are so afraid we cannot even go out to relieve ourselves?' These Hypocrites said the worst things about Him.

Before long, His promises were realized and Islam became victorious – because the Cause of Islam was assisted by heavenly forces. At the time of victory, these same Hypocrites were heard shouting, 'This is what God and His Messenger promised us!'

In this war there were only 700 fighters. Of these, some 300 were either Hypocrites or shaky and infirm in their faith. When they reached the palace of Khusraw[184] and perceived the tangible results of God's promise, they became ashamed and remorseful.[185]

'Abdu'l-Bahá was telling His audience that the sufferings of Bahá'u'lláh and His successive banishments would bring about great positive results in this world. He also mentioned that such an outcome was quite clear to those who have spiritual insight.

68

The Jews Broke Their Promise and Paid a Heavy Price

'How numerous the people who engaged in contests with Muḥammad, the Apostle of God, and were eventually reduced to naught . . .'[186]   The Báb

The Jews had made a pact with Muḥammad, promising to be of good behaviour in exchange for their protection by Him. Despite this, they collaborated with the Quraysh[187] and aligned troops against Islam. They besieged Muḥammad and His followers, who were forced to dig a moat. It so happened that one of the Jews[188] defected to the Muslim camp and caused a rift between the Jews and the Quraysh. This development helped to preserve Islam and protected it from their deceit. Some 700 of these enemies who had violated their contract were rooted out in one day. Otherwise, they would have again collaborated with other tribes to annihilate Islam.[189]

After relating this historical event, 'Abdu'l-Bahá said that the establishment of Islam and its preservation were very difficult under the prevailing conditions. He added that Islam is misjudged by those who do not know its history and are unaware of divine wisdom.

69

The Caliph's Donkey Returned to Town without Him

'O ye children of men! The fundamental purpose animating the Faith of God and His Religion is to safeguard the interests and promote the unity of the human race, and to foster the spirit of love and fellowship amongst men. Suffer it not to become a source of dissension and discord, of hate and enmity.'[190]

Bahá'u'lláh

Once al-Ḥákim bi'l-Amr[191] summoned to his presence some Jews and Christians and asked them, 'How long are you to wait for the coming of your promised one?'

They said, 'One hundred years.'

He pressed the issue and asked the same question again.

They answered, 'Four hundred years.'

Then he said, 'Four hundred years have passed and you are still denying.' He then decreed that a heavy collar in the shape of a cross be put on the neck of each Christian and that a pair of 100-gram earrings be worn by each Jew.

The poor Jews, with these heavy earrings, had to walk in the streets and whenever one's earlobe would become torn, his tormentors would make another hole in his ear and hang the weight again. Once they found a Jew whose ears were all torn and could not be pierced anymore.

One day al-Ḥákim went away, riding his donkey. After a while, the donkey returned without him. They searched and found his bloody shirt. It became known that his sister had had a hand in killing him. According to al-Ḥákim's decree, his sister ruled after him – until his son grew up and killed his own aunt.[192]

'Abdu'l-Bahá was explaining some events in the history of the Druze.

70

Ṭáhirih Offered to Show God to This Devout Muslim

'Say: He it is Who is the Manifestation of Him Who is the Unknowable, the Invisible of the Invisibles, could ye but perceive it.'[193]

Bahá'u'lláh

. . . Qurratu'l-'Ayn [Ṭáhirih] chanced to meet a devout Muhammadan who was praying and questioned him thus: 'To whom art thou praying, may I ask?' 'I am praying to the very Essence of Mercy and the Reality of Divinity.' And she, smiling, said: 'Oh, away with your god! Away with him! Your god is an imagination! Come, I will show you the God of today! It is the Báb! Your god is a phantom, while *this* is a certainty. Can the Sea be contained in a little glass?'[194]

'Abdu'l-Bahá was elaborating on the fact that man can direct his attention to God through His Manifestations. He remarked that all people worship their imaginary gods, which are superstitious phantoms.

71

The Báb Remembered God at All Times

'It is incumbent upon you to ponder in your hearts and meditate upon His words, and humbly to call upon Him, and to put away self in His heavenly Cause.'[195]

'Abdu'l-Bahá

His Holiness the Báb said, 'I worked in a commercial store at an early age. Whenever I had to write the address on a bale or read an address therefrom, I would lower my head and bow before God. In this way I had God in my mind, even in this small task. My goal was God and under all conditions He was in my view.'[196]

ʿAbduʾl-Bahá was advising the friends that they must always remember God in their daily activities.

72

A Prophet without a Green Turban?

'If we are lovers of the light, we adore it in whatever lamp it may become manifest, but if we love the lamp itself and the light is transferred to another lamp, we will neither accept nor sanction it.'[197] ʿAbduʾl-Bahá

At the time when the Bab was being driven by his enemies from place to place there lived in a certain city a believer who had never seen him. He had heard that the Bab wore a green turban, as did all the descendants of Muhammad. This believer went to see the Bab, and he looked for the green turban. It so happened that just before his arrival the Bab had taken off his green turban, putting on instead, a Persian cap. So the man did not recognize Him. The Bab joked, saying, 'I have heard that you have become a believer in the new movement. What has caused this change?'

The man answered: 'The proof of Muhammad was His eloquent Arabic book. I have heard that this young man has brought through revelation several eloquent Arabic and Persian epistles which have the spirit of the word of Muhammad.'

The Bab said: 'Whoever thus reveals, you believe?'

He then began writing verses, like a crystal river. The man, overwhelmed, cried out that such an one must be a Manifestation. 'But why does not he wear a green turban?'[198]

Here 'Abdu'l-Bahá was telling His audience that the Manifestations must be recognized by the attributes of God which are within them and not by their appearance, names and so on.

73

The Báb Did Not Compromise His Principles

'These holy Manifestations liberate the world of humanity from the imperfections which beset it and cause men to appear in the beauty of heavenly perfections.'[199]

'Abdu'l-Bahá

The merchants of Bushihr[200] practised dabbih. That is, the merchants, after having negotiated a transaction and agreed upon its terms, would ask for a reduction in the price at the time of payment. In this way, they would get some money back from the seller.

One day certain merchants went to the Báb and made an agreement for the purchase of a large amount of indigo. After this agreement, they carried the goods to their own store. When the time for payment arrived, they asked for a reduction in the price.

The Báb did not accept their request. He told them that they had already agreed upon the price and all other terms of the transaction, that the deal had been completed and so He refused to reduce the price. They insisted but the Báb remained firm.

They said, 'Dabbih is the custom of this land.'

The Báb answered, 'Soon many of these bad customs will be changed.'

No matter how much they insisted, the Báb did not change His position. He told them that if they thought that the price was too high, they could return the goods.

They repeated, 'Dabbih is customary among the people.'

The Báb said, 'I want to stop this custom.'

They went on, 'The goods have already been bought and transported to our store. Returning them would adversely affect our credit.'

His Holiness replied, 'It is up to you. You can complete the transaction but without dabbih.'

Again they mentioned the customary nature of dabbih and again He said, 'I will change this custom.'

Finally the Báb had the merchandise returned to Him, as he would not accept their request for dabbih. He also changed many other old-fashioned customs which were prevalent amongst the people.

Before too long one of the uncles of His Holiness arrived in Bushihr. The same merchants went to him and complained, 'He damaged our credit. We made a transaction and asked for a reduction in price but he refused. Then he had the merchandise returned to Him. This is a big insult to any merchant. You ought to advise Him to respect the will of the people and not to undermine their customs.'

The uncle said to His Holiness, 'Show regard for the people and the customs of the land.'

The Báb responded by saying, 'Even now, if they wish to effect another transaction and want to exercise dabbih, I will not accept it.'[201]

'Abdu'l-Bahá was talking to the pilgrims about the sojourn of the Báb in Bushihr and His work in that city.

74

He Did Not Believe Because the Báb was Martyred

'Yet all the divine Manifestations suffered, offered Their lives and blood, sacrificed Their existence, comfort and all They possessed for the sake of mankind.'[202]

'Abdu'l-Bahá

There was a Protestant who rejected the Bahá'í Faith because of the fact that His Holiness the Báb was martyred. He would say, 'If God is in this movement, why should He allow one of His chief agents to be put to death?'

He was answered, 'But how about the crucifixion of Christ?'

He responded, 'Oh, that is different.'[203]

'Abdu'l-Bahá was talking to the pilgrims about the difficulties that some religious people have in seeing the truth.

75

The Prime Minister Received a Lesson in the Qur'án

'The Heavenly Books, the Bible, the Qur'án, and the other Holy Writings have been given by God as guides into the paths of Divine virtue, love, justice and peace.'[204]   'Abdu'l-Bahá

. . . one day Mírzá Taqí Khán[205] attended a gathering (presumably in Ṭihrán) at which Bahá'u'lláh was present. He was referring to some verses of the Qur'án in a disrespectful manner and mockingly questioned the truth of the following verse:

He knoweth that which is on the dry land and in the sea; there falleth no leaf, but he knoweth it; neither is there a single grain in the dark parts of the earth, neither a green thing, nor a dry thing, but it is written in the perspicuous book [Qur'án].[206]

Bahá'u'lláh's immediate response was to disapprove the attitude of Mírzá Taqí Khán and to affirm that the above verse was undoubtedly true. When he asked for further

84

explanation, Bahá'u'lláh told him that it meant that the Qur'án was the repository of the Word of God; it contained various subjects such as history, commentaries, prophecies and so on. Within its pages were enshrined verities of great significance, and indeed one might discover that everything was mentioned in this Book.

'Am I mentioned in it?' asked Mírzá Taqí Khán arrogantly.

'Yes, you are,' was Bahá'u'lláh's prompt response.

'Am I alluded to or referred to clearly by name?' he asked.

'Clearly by name,' Bahá'u'lláh stated.

'It is strange', Mírzá Taqí Khán retorted with some degree of sarcasm, 'that I have not yet found a reference to myself in the Qur'án!'

'The reference to your name,' Bahá'u'lláh said, 'is in this verse: "She said, I fly for refuge unto the merciful from thee if thou art Taqi".'[207]

On hearing such a disparaging reference attributed to him by Bahá'u'lláh, Mírzá Taqí Khán became extremely angry, but did not reveal his anger. Instead he made a further attempt to ridicule the verse of the Qur'án in question and discredit Bahá'u'lláh. He asked, 'What about my father, Qurbán, is there a reference to him in the Qur'án also?'

'Yes, there is,' Bahá'u'lláh affirmed.

'Is he alluded to or referred to by name?' he asked.

'He is referred to by name in this verse,' responded Bahá'u'lláh, '". . . come unto us with the Qurbán[208] consumed by the fire".'[209]

Bahá'u'lláh always showed great respect for all the Prophets and He would not tolerate any discourteous reference to these holy individuals.

76

Bahá'u'lláh's Unique Possessions Were Indeed Priceless

'Cast away that which ye possess, and, on the wings of detachment, soar beyond all created things.'[210]

Bahá'u'lláh

Of all the precious belongings in Bahá'u'lláh's house, one of the things which was left for us was a rosary of pearl beads. At that time it was worth 10,000 túmáns. Each pearl was about the size of a filbert. Between every two adjoining pearls was inserted a piece of emerald. The tassel section, which was strung also with emerald beads, was about a finger long. It was something to behold. After everything was plundered, we were forced to mortgage those beads for a mere 1,000 túmáns. As the interest accumulated, we could not repossess the beads. In Paris today those beads would be worth 100,000 túmáns.

Another precious item was a book of Ḥáfiẓ's poetry which was in the handwriting of Mír 'Imád.[211] Muḥammad-Sháh sent for the book and asked about its price. The Blessed Beauty said, 'It has 12,000 lines, each line for one ashrafí (gold coin). So, it comes to 12,000 ashrafís.' The king's response was, 'With 12,000 ashrafís we can organize two military regiments.'

Another item was Du'áy-i-Kumayl,[212] which was written on deerskin. It was in the Kúfí style of writing and in the handwriting of Imám 'Alí. The notables of every century, including Mír 'Imád, had affixed their signatures on the book, certifying that the handwriting was that of Amír [Imám 'Alí]. This book was so rare and of such antiquity that it was truly priceless.

There were also plenty of jewels and precious items. All were gone. That book of Ḥáfiẓ and the handwriting of Amír fell into the possession of the prime minister, Mírzá

Áqá Khán. Two or three years ago the Bahá'ís had a great meeting in the mansion of that prime minister. From the early hours of the night until morning the cry of Yá Bahá'u'l-Abhá reached the lofty celestial sphere.

Despite all that wealth, we had absolutely nothing when we reached Baghdad. But, in any case, we did not pay much attention to the wealth of this world.[213]

Bahá'u'lláh sacrificed all His possessions and endured all hardships and ordeals for the betterment of the world.

77

Bahá'u'lláh Resided Where No One Dared to Approach

'Many a night We had no food for sustenance, and many a day Our body found no rest. By Him Who hath My being between His hands! notwithstanding these showers of afflictions and unceasing calamities, Our soul was wrapt in blissful joy, and Our whole being evinced an ineffable gladness.'[214]

Bahá'u'lláh

There was in Baghdad a man by the name of Ḥájí Faraj Kaḥḥál [oculist]. He himself used to say, 'I blinded three thousand eyes until at last I became an oculist.' This man frequented the Iranian Consulate and would take news to the Iranians. In those days, the *Tehran Gazette*, the first Iranian newspaper, was brought to the Consulate once every month. My uncle [Jináb-i-Kalím] would spend some time every day at the Ṣáliḥ coffeehouse which was located in the old section of Baghdad. He would also take me there and other Iranians would be there too.

One day Ḥájí Faraj related, 'It is reported in the paper that Áqá 'Abdu'l-Qásim-i-Hamadání went to Sulay-máníyyih. In Úrmán he was invited by its governor,

Ḥusayn-'Alí Khán. For his guest's safety, the governor sent several mounted guards with him. The guards took him by a wrong road to the top of a mountain. There they cut his throat and covered his body with rocks. Then they took all his possessions. Passing by the site of the crime, the residents of the nearby villages saw the blood on the ground. After some search, they exhumed the body and discovered that Áqá 'Abdu'l-Qásim was still alive. They took him to the village and stitched his throat. He could not talk but made known that he wanted paper and a pen. Then he wrote his own story:

"'I am Áqá 'Abdu'l-Qásim, a merchant from Hamadán. In Úrmán Ḥusayn-'Alí Khán invited me to his house. He then sent some people with me. They did this to me on the road and took all that I had. Now I want requital. They should return all my belongings which should be delivered to Darvísh Muḥammad-i-Irání who lives on Sar-Galú mountain. He is free to do with them whatever He wishes. I had returned to Iran from a visit to Him and was going back to Him again.'"

After hearing this story, we knew that this Dárvísh Muḥammad was the Blessed Beauty. In our respective homes, both Mírzá Áqá Ján and I repeated the supplication, 'O Thou Who art invoked!' 2,001 times. Then we asked Ḥájí Faraj if he knew of any other Iranians in Sulaymáníyyih. He said that there was one whose name was Ḥájí 'Abbás. Through Ḥájí Faraj we wrote to Ḥájí 'Abbás, who wrote back, 'This erudite dárvísh is residing on Sar-Galú mountain. It is impossible to go there because of the presence of hooligans. He comes to the town once a week to go to the public bath.'

Hence, Shaykh Sulṭán and Áqá Muḥammad Javád left for Sulaymáníyyih. There they investigated and made inquiries about His whereabouts. At last they learned that He was indeed residing on Sar-Galú mountain and that it was impossible for them to go there. So they waited in

Sulaymáníyyih until He arrived. They attended His presence and presented their plea. Bahá'u'lláh, however, did not agree. Then they said, 'We do not want to do anything contrary to Thy blessed will but we are not leaving Thy presence either.'[215]

This account was given by 'Abdu'l-Bahá as to how Bahá'u'lláh's presence in Sulaymáníyyih was discovered. It must be mentioned here that the pleas and supplications of Shaykh Sulṭán and Áqá Muḥammad Javád eventually paid off and Bahá'u'lláh agreed to return to Baghdad.

78

Two Could Have Defeated Thousands

'Shield us, then, O my God, from the mischief of Thine enemies, and assist us to help Thy Faith, and to protect Thy Cause, and to celebrate Thy glory.'[216]
Bahá'u'lláh

When the mujtahids[217] and Náṣiri'd-Dín Sháh sent Shaykh 'Abdu'l-Ḥusayn[218] to 'Iráq, and he began agitating against the Blessed Perfection (Bahá'u'lláh), the mujtahids gathered at Káẓimayn[219] to talk of waging a holy war, and they appealed to the Válí for help. When the Válí replied that he could not intervene, they sent letters to Baghdád, and a very large number of Persians and Shí'ih Arabs congregated there. Feelings in Baghdád came to the boil; they even sent for Shaykh Murtiḍá[220] to come from Karbílá, on the grounds that the welfare of their Faith was threatened. On his way to Baghdád, Shaykh Murtiḍá met with an accident; he held himself apart then and asked to be left alone. Because he had not personally investigated the matter, he refused to intervene. Through Zaynu'l-'Ábidín Khán, the Fakhru'd-Dawlih, the Shaykh sent this message to the

Blessed Perfection: 'I did not know; had I done so, I would not have come. Now I will pray for you.'

Those gathered in Kázimayn then arranged to come two days later and attack us. We were only forty-six in all, and our strong man was Áqá Asadu'lláh-i-Káshání, whose dagger, even when worn above his *shál* [the cloth used as a girdle], would dangle and touch the ground. Now there was a certain Siyyid Ḥasan from Shíráz. He was not a believer, but he was a very good man. One morning, when the Blessed Perfection had been up and about, this Áqá Siyyid Ḥasan came knocking at our door. Our black maid opened the door, Áqá Siyyid Ḥasan came in and, much agitated, asked, 'Where is the Áqá [Bahá'u'lláh]?' I said, 'He has gone to the riverside.' 'What is it that you say?' he responded. I offered him tea and said, 'He will come back.' He replied, 'Áqá! The world has been turned upside down . . . It has become turbulent . . . Do you know that last night they held a council in the presence of Shaykh 'Abdu'l-Ḥusayn and the Consul? They have also reached some sort of agreement with the Válí. How is it that the Blessed Perfection has gone to the riverside? They have decided to start their attack tomorrow.' Whilst he was telling me what had happened, the Blessed Perfection came in. Áqá Siyyid Ḥasan wanted immediately to express his anxiety. But the Blessed Perfection said, 'Let us talk of other matters', and went on speaking. Later, Áqá Siyyid Ḥasan insisted on unburdening himself. However, the Blessed Perfection told him, 'It is of no consequence.' So Áqá Siyyid Ḥasan stayed for lunch and then went home.

Late in the afternoon the Blessed Perfection came out. The friends gathered round Him. Amongst them were two who were double-faced: Ḥájí 'Abdu'l-Ḥamíd and Áqá Muḥammad-Javád-i-Iṣfahání. The Blessed Perfection was walking up and down. Then He turned to the Friends and said, 'Have you heard the news? The mujtahids and the Consul have come together and gathered ten to twenty

thousand people round them to wage *jihád* against Us.'
Then He addressed the two double-faced men, 'Go and tell
them, by the One God, the Lord of all, I will send two men
to drive them away, all the way to Kázimayn. If they are
capable of accepting a challenge, let them come.'

The two hurried away and repeated what they had
heard. And do you know, they dispersed![221]

An event in the life of Bahá'u'lláh while He was residing in Baghdad.

79

People Just Would Not Pay Any Attention to the Shaykh

*'It is evident and manifest unto every discerning observer that even as the light
of the star fadeth before the effulgent splendour of the sun, so doth the lumi-
nary of earthly knowledge, of wisdom, and understanding vanish into
nothingness when brought face to face with the resplendent glories of the Sun
of Truth, the Day-star of divine enlightenment.'[222]*   Bahá'u'lláh

During the days of Baghdad and Sulaymáníyyih, Shaykh
'Abdu'l-Husayn[223] commented that the Blessed Beauty had
succeeded in attracting the Kurds by explaining Sufi terminology and expressions. The poor Shaykh searched and
found a copy of *al-Futu'hát al-Makkiyyah*[224] and committed its
verses to memory. But wherever he recited them, nobody
listened. He was quite surprised at this lack of interest. The
Blessed Beauty said, 'Tell the Shaykh that We do not read
al-Futu'hát al-Makkiyyah but infuse the verses of civilization.
We do not talk about the *Fusus* of the Shaykh but utter the
words of God.'[225]

*'Abdu'l-Bahá was telling the friends that speech must be suited to the audi-
ence and the occasion.*

80

The Shaykh Learned the True Meaning of His Dream

'Bahá'u'lláh promulgated the fundamental oneness of religion: He taught that reality is one and not multiple, that it underlies all divine precepts and that the foundations of the religions are, therefore, the same.'[226]   'Abdu'l-Bahá

One night, Shaykh 'Abdu'l-Ḥusayn the mujtahid told his cohorts about a dream he had. 'In my dream', he said, 'I saw the king of Iran sitting under a dome. He said to me, "O Shaykh, be certain of this, that my sword will eliminate the Bahá'ís altogether." On that dome, under which the king was sitting, was written the Ayatu'l-Kursí[227] in English.'

The Blessed Beauty sent him the following message through Zaynu'l-'Abidín Khán, Fakhru'd-Dawlih, 'Your dream is a prophetic one, because Ayatu'l-Kursí is the very same verse as in the Qur'án, although written in English. It means that this Faith is the same as Islam but the script has changed. That is, the words are different but the reality and the true meaning remain the same. As regards that dome, it signifies the Cause of God, which is surrounding and over-seeing the king. The king is in the shelter of the divine Cause, which is truly victorious.'[228]

The progress of the Cause was the theme of 'Abdu'l-Bahá's talk. After telling this story, He said, 'Now, where is that King or the Shaykh to see that such a large gathering has assembled under this canopy in Port Sa'id, Egypt . . .'

81

The 'Ulamá Wanted a Miracle to Convince Them

'Say: Already have apostles before me come to you with miracles, and with

that of which you speak. Wherefore slew ye them? Tell me, if ye are men of truth.[229]

Muḥammad

It often happened that in Bag͟hdád certain Muḥammadan 'ulamá, Jewish rabbis and Christians met together with some European scholars, in a blessed reunion: each one had some question to propose, and although they were possessed of varying degrees of culture, they each heard a sufficient and convincing reply, and retired satisfied. Even the Persian 'ulamá who were at Karbilá and Najaf chose a wise man whom they sent on a mission to Him; his name was Mullá Ḥasan 'Amú. He came into the Holy Presence, and proposed a number of questions on behalf of the 'ulamá, to which Bahá'u'lláh replied. Then Ḥasan 'Amú said, 'The 'ulamá recognize without hesitation and confess the knowledge and virtue of Bahá'u'lláh, and they are unanimously convinced that in all learning he has no peer or equal; and it is also evident that he has never studied or acquired this learning; but still the 'ulamá say, "We are not contented with this; we do not acknowledge the reality of his mission by virtue of his wisdom and righteousness. Therefore, we ask him to show us a miracle in order to satisfy and tranquillize our hearts."'

Baha'u'llah replied, 'Although you have no right to ask this, for God should test His creatures, and they should not test God, still I allow and accept this request. But the Cause of God is not a theatrical display that is presented every hour, of which some new diversion may be asked for every day. If it were thus, the Cause of God would become mere child's play.

'The 'ulamás must, therefore, assemble, and, with one accord, choose one miracle, and write that, after the performance of this miracle they will no longer entertain doubts about Me, and that all will acknowledge and confess the truth of My Cause. Let them seal this paper, and bring it to Me. This must be the accepted criterion: if the miracle is performed, no doubt will remain for them; and if not, We shall be convicted of imposture.' The learned man, Ḥasan 'Amú, rose and replied, 'There is no more to be said'; he then kissed the knee of the Blessed One although he was not a believer, and went. He gathered the 'ulamá and gave them the sacred message. They consulted together and said, 'This man is an enchanter; perhaps he will perform an enchantment, and then we shall have nothing more to say.' Acting on this belief, they did not dare to push the matter further.

This man, Ḥasan 'Amú, mentioned this fact at many meetings. After leaving Karbilá he went to Kirmánsháh and Ṭihrán and spread a detailed account of it everywhere, laying emphasis on the fear and the withdrawal of the 'ulamá.[230]

This is part of 'Abdu'l-Bahá's talk on the life of Bahá'u'lláh.

82

Mírzá Muḥíṭ Lost the Life He Cherished So Much

'Seize, O friends, the chance which this Day offereth you, and deprive not yourselves of the liberal effusions of His grace.'[231]　　　Bahá'u'lláh

When the Blessed Beauty was in Baghdad, Mírzá Muḥíṭ, the famous Shaykhí,[232] arrived in that city for the purpose of visiting Káẓimayn. A great grandson of Fatḥ-'Alí Sháh, Kayván Mírzá, would at times visit Bahá'u'lláh. Mírzá Muḥíṭ went to this prince and asked him to go to Bahá'u'lláh and say that Mírzá Muḥíṭ wanted to visit Him in absolute secrecy.

He continued his instructions to the prince, 'No one, even those around His Holiness such as His attendants and relatives, should know of this. You and only you are to know of this visit, which should take place at midnight. When I arrive from Kázimayn I will go directly to your house and at midnight we will proceed from there to His blessed presence.

Kayván Mírzá went to Bahá'u'lláh and related Mírzá Muḥíṭ's wish for a visit with those conditions.

The Blessed Beauty said, 'Tell Mírzá Muḥíṭ that in the days of My retirement in Sulaymáníyyih I composed a certain ode, a part of which reads: "If thine aim be to cherish thy life, approach not our court; but if sacrifice be thy heart's desire, come and let others come with thee. For such is the way of Faith, if in thy heart thou seekest reunion with Bahá; should thou refuse to tread this path, why trouble us? Be gone!"'

Kayván Mírzá conveyed this message to Mírzá Muḥíṭ, who did not come.

The following day Mírzá Muḥíṭ rode directly to Karbalá. On the third day he developed a fever and became delirious. On the seventh day he died. The intervening time between the answer of the Blessed Beauty and the death of Mírzá Muḥíṭ was one week.[233]

'Abdu'l-Bahá was talking to the pilgrims about past events.

83

He Became a Bábí Before the Declaration of the Báb

'None have believed in Him except them who, through the power of the Lord of Names, have shattered the idols of their vain imaginings and corrupt desires and entered the city of certitude.'[234]   Bahá'u'lláh

'When the Bahais were living in Bagdad there was a very prominent man who used often to come to see Baha-Ullah [Bahá'u'lláh]. He sat in His Presence with the greatest respect and listened attentively to his utterances. One day he tried to express his faith and belief in the Cause with all apparent sincerity and devotion. "Yes, my Lord!" he concluded his talk, "I thoroughly believe in this Cause. In the year 1830, one of the great teachers of this Movement passed by our city. I met him and he talked with me for several days and his words convinced me of the validity of this revelation. From that time on I have been a believer." . . . this man did not know that the movement was inaugurated only in 1844 and so, in order to convince Baha-Ullah of the genuineness of his belief, he had set the time of his acceptance 14 years before the declaration of the Bab![235]

'Abdu'l-Bahá was talking to a group of friends about individuals who claimed to be Bahá'ís in the hope of some material reward.

84

The Dervish Was Beaten but Showed Resignation

'By the righteousness of God! He is fully capable of revolutionizing the world through the power of a single Word. Having enjoined upon all men to observe wisdom, He Himself hath adhered to the cord of patience and resignation.'[236]

Bahá'u'lláh

When Baha-Ullah [Bahá'u'lláh] with his family were leaving Bagdad, a dervish[dárvi_sh_] begged Abdul Baha's permission to join the party. He was told that the trip would be most difficult, but the Dervish was willing to accept all manner of hardships so he travelled with the party as far as Constantinople. Then when they left for Adrianople, he stayed behind, but joined them later, for having become accustomed to associate with the Bahais, he could not live without them. In Adrianople, he rented a room in an adjoining Mosque with another friend, and for some time they lived together peacefully. One day the Dervish came to

Baha-Ullah saying: 'My friend attacked me this morning and gave me a sound beating, but I said nothing. I was in a state of utmost resignation. Then after half an hour he returned, kissed my hands and said, 'Verily, you have attained the state of great merit, you are now a saint.' Baha-Ullah, listening with interest to this story, said laughingly: 'If he beats you another time and you demonstrate such resignation, he may believe that you have attained the Station of Prophethood.'[237]

'Abdu'l-Bahá was entertaining a few of the Bahá'ís in His company in Egypt.

85

This Father Got His Wish and Snared His Bird of Joy

'Rejoice for the glance of the Blessed Beauty, Bahá'u'lláh, is directed upon you. Rejoice for Bahá'u'lláh is your protector.'[238]
'Abdu'l-Bahá

Another of those who left their homes and came to settle in the neighbourhood of Bahá'u'lláh was Ḥájí Muḥammad Khán. This distinguished man, a native of Sístán, was a Balúch. When he was very young, he caught fire and became a mystic – an 'áríf, or adept. As a wandering dervish, completely selfless, he went out from his home and, following the dervish rule, travelled about in search of his murshid, his perfect leader . . . Thus at the very moment when he heard the call from the Kingdom of God, he shouted, 'Yea, verily!' and he was off like the desert wind. He travelled over vast distances, arrived at the Most Great Prison and attained the presence of Bahá'u'lláh. When his eyes fell upon that bright Countenance he was instantly enslaved. He returned to Persia so that he could meet with those people who professed to be following the Path, those friends of other days who were seeking out the Truth, and deal with them as his loyalty and duty required . . . He reached his homeland and set his family's affairs in order, providing for all, seeing to the security, happiness and comfort of each one. After that he bade them all goodby. To his relatives, his wife, children, kin, he said: 'Do not look for me again; do not wait for my return.'

He took up a staff and wandered away; over the mountains he went, across the plains, seeking and finding the mystics, his friends. On his first journey, he went to the late Mírzá Yúsuf Khán (Mustawfíyu'l-Mamálik), in Ṭihrán. When he had said his say, Yúsuf Khán expressed a wish, and declared that should it be fulfilled, he would believe; the wish was to be given a son. Should such a bounty become his, Yúsuf Khán would be won over. The Ḥájí reported this to Bahá'u'lláh, and received a firm promise in reply. Accordingly, when the Ḥájí met with Yúsuf Khán on his second journey, he found him with a child in his arms. 'Mírzá,' the Ḥájí cried, 'praise be to God! Your test has demonstrated the Truth. You snared your bird of joy.' 'Yes,' answered Yúsuf Khán, 'the proof is clear. I am convinced. This year, when you go to Bahá'u'lláh, say that I implore His grace and favour for this child, so that it may be kept safe in the sheltering care of God.'[239]

That same child is now his eminence, the minister.

Part of 'Abdu'l-Bahá's account of the life of Ḥájí Muḥammad Khán.

86

The Sincere Pleadings of This Resolute Mufti Paid Off

'And among His signs is the sublimity of His grandeur, His exalted state, His

towering glory, and the shining out of His beauty above the horizon of the Prison . . .'[240]

'Abdu'l-Bahá

In 'Akká the first person to throw himself at the feet of Bahá'u'lláh and kiss His garment was its Mufti.[241] Whatever we did to get the Blessed Beauty to move to the garden [mansion of Mazra'ih] was of no avail. He would not accept it. He would say, 'We are prisoners and a prisoner should be confined.' At last I went to the Mufti, who was a highly respected and resolute person. I said to him, 'Can you do something so that perhaps the Blessed Beauty will leave [the barracks]?' Since he was sincere and a pure soul, he got up immediately and went directly to Bahá'u'lláh. After obtaining permission, he attended His presence and threw himself at His feet, saying, 'I have a wish and I will not get up until you grant it.' He went on insisting and pleading until at last Bahá'u'lláh granted his wish. Bahá'u'lláh then left the barracks and went to Mazra'ih where everything had been made ready for His auspicious arrival.[242]

The discussion was about the greatness of the Cause and the grandeur of Bahá'u'lláh. 'Abdu'l-Bahá said that although Bahá'u'lláh was a prisoner, no one could attend His presence without first obtaining His permission.

87

His Boxed God Vanished

'The essence of wealth is love for Me; whoso loveth Me is the possessor of all things, and he that loveth Me not is indeed of the poor and needy.'[243]

Bahá'u'lláh

Muḥammad-Javád had a brother in Istanbul who was supplicating and entreating God to become rich. The Blessed Beauty prayed on his behalf and promised him prosperity.

After this, it so happened that much of the cotton stored in Paris caught fire and burned up. Since this man was trading in cotton, his business soared. After he attained his goal and became wealthy, he forgot all.

The Blessed Beauty sent someone to Istanbul to see why there was no news of him. When he was contacted, he said to the envoy, 'God is in this box,' meaning that God is money.

The envoy returned and reported the situation to the Blessed Beauty, who then became very sad. He said, 'We will take it from him the same way We gave it to him.'

Before long he lost all his wealth and repented on His threshold.

The Blessed Beauty forgave him on the condition that he go to Bákú[244] and transcribe the revealed Tablets. He went there and spent his time in transcribing. At the end, he died in poverty.[245]

On becoming rich, man also becomes rebellious.

88

Mírzá Ja'far Was Dead but Came Alive Again

'Thy name is my healing, O my God, and remembrance of Thee is my remedy.'[246]
Bahá'u'lláh

On the journey from 'Iráq to Constantinople, Mírzá Ja'far[247] was one of Bahá'u'lláh's retinue, and in seeing to the needs of the friends, he was a partner to this servant. When we would come to a stopping-place the believers, exhausted by the long hours of travel, would rest or sleep. Mírzá Ja'far and I would go here and there to the surrounding villages to find oats, straw and other provisions for the caravan. Since there was a famine in that area, it sometimes happened that we would be roaming from village to village from after the noon hour until half the night was gone. As best we could, we would procure whatever was available, then return to the convoy.

Mírzá Ja'far was patient and long-suffering, a faithful attendant at the Holy Threshold. He was a servant to all the friends, working day and night. A quiet man, sparing of speech, in all things relying entirely upon God. He continued to serve in Adrianople until the banishment to 'Akká was brought about and he too was made a prisoner. He was grateful for this, continually offering thanks, and saying, 'Praise be to God! I am in the fully-laden Ark!'

The Prison was a garden of roses to him, and his narrow cell a wide and fragrant place. At the time when we were in the barracks he fell dangerously ill and was confined to his bed. He suffered many complications, until finally the doctor gave him up and would visit him no more. Then the sick man breathed his last. Mírzá Áqá Ján ran to Bahá'u'lláh, with word of the death. Not only had the patient ceased to breathe, but his body was already going limp. His family were gathered about him, mourning him, shedding bitter tears. The Blessed Beauty said, 'Go; chant the prayer of Yá Sháfi – O Thou, the Healer – and Mírzá Ja'far will come alive. Very rapidly, he will be as well as ever.' I reached his bedside. His body was cold and all the signs of death were present. Slowly, he began to stir; soon he could move his limbs, and before an hour had passed he lifted his head, sat up, and proceeded to laugh and tell jokes.

He lived for a long time after that, occupied as ever with serving the friends.[248]

This is part of 'Abdu'l-Bahá's account of the life of this early believer.

89

'Abdu'l-Bahá Walked 12 Miles to a Thorn-Picker's Hut

'O ye friends of mine! Illumine the meeting with the light of the love of God, make it joyful and happy through the melody of the Kingdom of holiness, and with heavenly food and through the "Lord's Supper" confer life.'[249]

'Abdu'l-Bahá

Once, when I lived in Baghdad . . . I was invited to the house of a poor thorn-picker. In Baghdad the heat is greater even than in Syria; and it was a very hot day. But I walked twelve miles to the thorn-picker's hut. Then his wife made a little cake out of some meal for Me and burnt it in cooking it, so that it was a black, hard lump. Still that was the best reception I ever attended.[250]

The Master was telling those in His company that a building becomes special to Him if a good believer lives in it.

90

The Sultan's Decree Soon Became Ineffective

'My body hath borne imprisonment that your souls may be released from bondage, and We have consented to be abased that ye may be exalted. Follow the Lord of glory and dominion, and not every ungodly oppressor.'[251]

Bahá'u'lláh

When we first arrived in 'Akká and entered the army barracks, the government authorities informed us one day that an individual representing Bahá'u'lláh should go and hear the Sultan's farmán. The Blessed Beauty sent me to Government House as His representative. First they put me where the guilty ones are placed. Then the public speaker went behind a podium and read the royal decree, which was in Turkish. In essence, it said that the family of Bahá'u'lláh would be imprisoned in 'Akká forever and that they would not have the right to leave the city. After hearing this edict I laughed. Those present were quite surprised and asked me, 'Why do you laugh?' I said, 'This passage has no meaning. If we are to remain in the city forever, we must also live forever. But we are not going to live eternally.' By fate, this farmán was later nullified because Bahá'u'lláh passed through the city gate and came up this very mountain – Carmel. I, too, left the city through its gate and went to Beirut.[252]

The discussion was about the persecution of the Persian believers.

91

A Little Dog Put Five Big Dogs to Shame

'By the might of my Lord, verily, the Lord will assist only those who will remain firm in His Cause, and desire union, love, humility and submissiveness, and to become separated from aught else save God.'[253]

'Abdu'l-Bahá

We were at Acca ['Akká] when Kamel Pasha became Prime Minister. His brother became the Governor of Acca. In Turkey the brother of the Prime Minister can do whatever he wishes. No one can object to him. One day he came with a carriage and we went out together. On the way I noticed he had a hunting outfit and he had four or five large hunting dogs. A gazelle was sighted. These dogs chased after it.

One of the Bahais had a small dog. An Arab Bahai. He also had come. These five dogs of the Governor did not catch anything. This little dog caught a large gazelle. The

Governor became ashamed. When the dogs returned, he began to beat them. He said: 'What can I do, the Bahais are assisted! These five large dogs of mine could catch nothing, but this little dog did.' He dismounted and took the little dog in his arms and kissed it. He told the owner of the dog that he would not give the dog back to him.[254]

'Abdu'l-Bahá was talking to the pilgrims about the successful teaching activities of Miss Alma Knobloch, a Bahá'í who was physically very small.

92

At the Right Time, 'Abdu'l-Bahá's Malady Disappeared

'Glorified art Thou, O my God! I implore Thee by the Dawning-Place of Thy signs and by the Revealer of Thy clear tokens to grant that I may, under all conditions, hold fast the cord of Thy loving providence and cling tenaciously to the hem of Thy generosity.'[255] Bahá'u'lláh

I was a child in Tehran when at the age of seven I contracted tuberculosis. There was no hope of recovery. The wisdom of this sickness became clear later. If I had not been ill, I would have been obliged to go to Mázindarán but because of this sickness I stayed in Tehran. This was when the Blessed Beauty was in prison in Tehran. Therefore, I was afforded the honour of being in His company during His journey to Iraq. When the right time arrived, I suddenly became well, after the doctors had given up all hope of recovery.[256]

'Abdu'l-Bahá said, 'There is a profound wisdom in whatever transpires.'

93

'Abdu'l-Bahá Knew Arabic Better Than Any Learned Arab

'Verily, I pray my Lord to teach thee a language and writing of the Kingdom which will satisfy thee, so as to dispense with all things; for that spiritual writing and instructive tongue are eloquent, clear, laudable, legible, read by the tongue and preserved in the heart.'[257]

'Abdu'l-Bahá

I did not study Arabic. When I was a child I had a book of prayers by the Báb in the handwriting of the Blessed Beauty. I was very eager to read it. Whenever I would wake up in the middle of the night, I would get up, read it and would cry from sheer excitement. Eventually I realized that I understood Arabic very well. My old friends know well that I never attended any schools. But I know the Arabic language better than any eloquent Arab.[258]

'Abdu'l-Bahá was praising the ability of an American lady who could speak Persian. He encouraged her to read and learn Bahá'u'lláh's poems in the Persian language.

94

'Abdu'l-Bahá Found the Governor's Ring

'By my life! Neither the pomp of the mighty, nor the wealth of the rich, nor even the ascendancy of the ungodly will endure. All will perish, at a word from Him.'[259]

Bahá'u'lláh

When Ra__sh__íd Pá__sh__á[260] came to Haifa, I did not pay much attention to him. Ra__sh__íd Pá__sh__á even sent his son to 'Akká and contrived other plans to extract a bribe but all came to nothing. Once more he came to Haifa and through the mediation of the Governor of 'Akká I was called to that city. He hinted much here and there but I paid no attention whatsoever. There were no gifts or bribes to be had from us. It so happened, however, that on that same day the Governor of 'Akká lost his expensive ring on the way to Haifa.

On the way back to 'Akká he told me about it. I told him that he should not worry about it and that it would be found. When we reached 'Akká, I disembarked near the shop of a goldsmith. I went to him and said that such a ring would be brought to him. I told him that he should take it and bring it to me immediately. Then I joined the Governor in the carriage and we continued our return trip home.

The following morning the goldsmith brought that very ring to me. I took it and gave it to the Governor, who was quite perplexed. Then he went to Rashíd Páshá and said, "Abbás Effendi knows the system of divination of our Master 'Alí.[261] My ring was lost but He found it so easily. Therefore you must desist from disturbing Him, for He freely states that if the whole world assembled and tried to secure His release from prison before the appointed time, it would be impossible. He also says that when the time for His liberation does arrive, if all the monarchs of the world unite they will be unable to interfere with His liberty.'

Since Rashíd Páshá had total confidence in the Governor, he did for some time cease his aggression and halt his greed.[262]

When 'Abdu'l-Bahá was in Paris the arrogant Rashíd Páshá paid Him a humble visit in His residence. That evening 'Abdu'l-Bahá related this story to the friends.

95

The Father Had an Alarming Dream about His Daughter

'Behold how the dream thou hast dreamed is, after the lapse of many years, re-enacted before thine eyes.'[263]   Bahá'u'lláh

In 'Akká [I] was visited by a Christian who expressed his disbelief in dreams. [I] said, '. . . your own Sacred Writings mention such things.'

'Still the man remained sceptical. A few months later, however, he reappeared in 'Akká, went on his knees, and confessed his belief in dreams. Through a sorrowful experience he had learned that what I had told him was true. The man explained that one night when he was away from home he had had an alarming dream of his little daughter. She had come to him, sat on his knee and complained that her head ached. Rapidly she grew worse. They sent for the doctor. The father knew in his dream that she was hopelessly ill and felt the most acute anguish. Then he saw her die. The following night he returned to his home and his daughter came and sat on his knee. 'Father,' she said, 'my head aches.' Then followed her illness, her death.[264]

'Abdu'l-Bahá told those with Him that there were three kinds of dreams: dreams coming from bodily disorders, those which are symbolic and ones which foretell future events.

96

He Kept His Old Mat and Sold the Soft Persian Rug

'Bestow My wealth upon My poor, that in heaven thou mayest draw from stores of unfading splendour and treasures of imperishable glory.'[265]

Bahá'u'lláh

One day in Baghdad a poor man came to our house. He saw the Persian rug which was on the floor. He rubbed it with his hands and said, 'It is very soft. One can sleep better on this. It must be very comfortable.' I told him that he could have the rug. After a while I saw him again. He said, 'I thought that I could have a better and longer sleep on the rug. Now I know that there is no difference between sleeping on a rug or on a mat. Therefore I sold the rug.'[266]

After returning from a gathering which was for the benefit of the poor people of Edinburgh, 'Abdu'l-Bahá talked to a few friends about the importance of kindness to the needy and the appalling conditions of the poor people in the East.

97

Ḥajjáj's Wife Didn't Think that He Was So Great

'Cast away, therefore, the mere conceit thou dost follow, for mere conceit can never take the place of truth.'[267]

Bahá'u'lláh

There was a man by the name of Muṣṭafá Beg, who was the office manager of the Mufti[268] of 'Akká. He was a corrupt and unattractive person who showed much hatred towards the Faith.

One night we were invited to the Mufti's house. Muṣṭafá Beg was also there. At one point I related a story about

Ḥajjáj ibn-i Yúsuf. 'Ḥajjáj', I said, 'had a wife who was very beautiful and who did not like Ḥajjáj at all. One day Ḥajjáj, while looking at himself in the mirror, said, "O God, you created me with such outer and inner beauty." His wife told him that he was falsely accusing God.

'The following morning Muṣṭafá Beg was looking in the mirror. The Mufti said to him, "Say, O God, you created me with such outer and inner beauty."

'As soon as the Mufti said that, there was an outburst of laughter.'[269]

'Abdu'l-Bahá was talking to the pilgrims about some government officials who were greedy and were set against the Faith. Muṣṭafá Beg was eventually removed from office and requested 'Abdu'l-Bahá's assistance in his personal affairs. 'Abdu'l-Bahá helped him very generously.

98

The Poor Camel Was Eventually Rescued

'Bring them [children] up to work and strive, and accustom them to hardship. Teach them to dedicate their lives to matters of great import, and inspire them to undertake studies that will benefit mankind.'[270]   'Abdu'l-Bahá

One day in the company of the Governor, the judge and the commander of the military, I was returning to 'Akká from its outskirts. On the way home we saw a camel which had fallen into a ditch and was stuck. The animal was going to die and the camel driver could do nothing but cry.

I collected about a hundred friends to help but no matter how hard they tried, they couldn't rescue the camel. Then a few Bedouin Arabs who were passing by answered our call and came to the rescue. They freed the animal with ease, despite the fewness of their number. This was possible because they were experienced and hard-working people.[271]

'Abdu'l-Bahá was talking about the training of children. He said that it would be very beneficial to children if they were accustomed to hardship early in their life. He also said that it would be better if they were not protected too much from heat and cold.

99

Cooperation is Practised Even among the Insects

'There is brotherhood natal in mankind because all are elements of one human society subject to the necessity of agreement and cooperation. There is brotherhood intended in humanity because all are waves of one sea, leaves and fruit of one tree.'[272]
'Abdu'l-Bahá

One day I was standing by a creek and observed that a swarm of small locusts whose wings had not yet developed wanted to go to the other side of the creek to find food. To make this possible for them, some of the adult locusts rushed forward, each one trying to get ahead of the others. They threw themselves into the water to establish a bridge from one side of the creek to the other. Then the small ones crossed the creek by walking on this bridge.

All the locusts that formed this bridge lost their own lives in this process.[273]

'Abdu'l-Bahá was talking about the necessity of cooperation among all the peoples of the world. He told this story to show that cooperation is practised even among the animals.

100

He Was Inflated with Pride and Got a Broken Leg

'As to him who turneth aside, and swelleth with pride, after that the clear

tokens have come unto him, from the Revealer of signs, his work shall God bring to naught.'[274]

Baháʾuʾlláh

In Haifa there was at one time a German Consul who became [my] friend. He used to call on [me] often, and [I] returned his visits. At one time, he disappeared for a whole month. Suddenly, one day he entered [my] room. He had a stick in his hand and was lame. 'Oh, sir, how is it that you have not inquired about my health during the past month?' 'Why, friend, what has happened to thee?' 'Yes,' he pitifully answered, 'I am the victim of "Bravo". Let me tell you how it happened. The German Colony had prepared a ball, to which I was bidden. The governor, the judges and the officials of Haifa were likewise invited. When the dancing was over, they had a jumping contest. One by one they started to jump, but in a clumsy manner. I saw that none of them had learned the art of jumping a long distance, but I had learned it in boyhood, going to a gymnasium in Germany. When the last one failed to reach the mark, I volunteered as a candidate. All eyes were on me now. My first attempt was so successful that it elicited the hearty "Bravo" of the governor. In my heart I was pleased and thought I would try again, and go beyond the first limit. I went back and back, then jumped forward, and when I landed on the other side, a tumultuous applause was raised from the governor and the officials. "Bravo, bravo" rang in my ears. By this time I was puffed up with pride and became blind to my own limitations. "Now I will show them," I said to myself, "what real jumping is," and with this determination I started the third time. I wanted to go further, much further than the first and second time, and so, when I came down upon the earth with a great crash, I felt a most excruciating pain in my right foot. My leg was broken. I became unconscious, and when I opened my eyes, I found myself in bed. For the last thirty days I have suffered much. Thus you see now, how I became the victim of the "Bravos" of the governor.'[275]

This story illustrates that some people believe the chatter of flatterers, become proud and eventually come to a sad end.

101

The Same Food Produced Such Different Results

'*The All-Knowing Physician hath His finger on the pulse of mankind. He perceiveth the disease, and prescribeth, in His unerring wisdom, the remedy. Every age hath its own problem, and every soul its particular aspiration. The remedy the world needeth in its present-day afflictions can never be the same as that which a subsequent age may require.*'[276]   Bahá'u'lláh

Yet one more among those who emigrated and came to settle near Bahá'u'lláh was the bookbinder, Muḥammad-Hádí. This noted man was from Iṣfáhán, and as a binder and illuminator of books he had no peer. When he gave himself up to the love of God he was alert on the path and fearless. He abandoned his home and began a dreadful journey, passing with extreme hardship from one country to another until he reached the Holy Land and became a prisoner. He stationed himself by the Holy Threshold, carefully sweeping it and keeping watch. Through his constant efforts, the square in front of Bahá'u'lláh's house was at all times swept, sprinkled and immaculate . . .

One day he came to me and complained of a chronic ailment. 'I have suffered from chills and fever for two years,' he said. 'The doctors have prescribed a purgative, and quinine. The fever stops a few days; then it returns. They give me more quinine, but still the fever returns. I am weary of this life, and can no longer do my work. Save me!'

'What food would you most enjoy?' I asked him. 'What would you eat with great appetite?'

'I don't know,' he said.

Jokingly, I named off the different dishes. When I came to barley soup with whey (ásh-i-kashk), he said, 'Very good! But on condition there is braised garlic in it.'

I directed them to prepare this for him, and I left. The next day he presented himself and told me: 'I ate a whole bowlful of the soup. Then I laid my head on my pillow and slept peacefully till morning.'

In short, from then on he was perfectly well for about two years.

One day a believer came to me and said: 'Muḥammad-Hádí is burning up with fever.' I hurried to his bedside and found him with a fever of 42° Centigrade. He was barely conscious. 'What has he done?' I asked. 'When he became feverish', was the reply, 'he said that he knew from experience what he should do. Then he ate his fill of barley soup with whey and braised garlic; and this was the result.'

I was astounded at the workings of fate. I told them: 'Because, two years ago, he had been thoroughly purged and his system was clear; because he had a hearty appetite for it, and his ailment was fever and chills, I prescribed the barley soup. But this time, with the different foods he has had, with no appetite, and especially with a high fever, there was no reason to diagnose the previous chronic condition. How could he have eaten the soup!' They answered, 'It was fate.' Things had gone too far; Muḥammad-Hádí was past saving.[277]

This is part of 'Abdu'l-Bahá's account of the life of this greatly tested believer.

102

Nobody Could Hear the Thief Playing His Trumpet

'All the people of the world are buried in the graves of nature, or are slumbering, heedless and unaware. Just as Christ saith: 'I may come when you are not aware. The coming of the Son of Man is like the coming of a thief into a house, the owner of which is utterly unaware.'[278]　'Abdu'l-Bahá

There is a Persian story of a thief who, in order to rob a certain house, went to work to undermine the foundations. The owner of the house happened to be on the roof and looking down discovered the thief and asked what he was doing. The man replied, 'I am trumpeting.' 'Trumpeting!' exclaimed the owner. 'Why are you not making any noise?' 'Oh no,' answered the thief, 'you will hear the noise tomorrow.'[279]

The message of a Manifestation is not heard or heeded at first.

103

The Rabbi Made His Audience Extremely Happy

'Behold how the people, as a result of the verdict pronounced by the divines of His age, have cast Abraham, the Friend of God, into fire; how Moses, He Who held converse with the Almighty, was denounced as liar and slanderer. Reflect how Jesus, the Spirit of God, was, notwithstanding His extreme meekness and perfect tender-heartedness, treated by His enemies.'[280]

Bahá'u'lláh

I was once at Tiberias where the Jews have a Temple. I was staying in a house just opposite the Temple, and there I saw and heard a Rabbi speaking to his congregation of Jews, and he spoke thus:

'O Jews, you are in truth the people of God! All other races and religions are of the devil. God has created you the descendants of Abraham, and He has showered His blessings upon you. Unto you God sent Moses, Jacob and Joseph, and many other great prophets. These prophets, one and all, were of your race.

'It was for you that God broke the power of Pharaoh and caused the Red Sea to dry up; to you also He sent manna from above to be your food, and out of the stony rock did He give you water to quench your thirst. You are indeed the chosen people of God, you are above all the races of the earth! Therefore, all other races are abhorrent to God, and condemned by Him. In truth you will govern and subdue the world, and all men shall become your slaves.

'Do not profane yourselves by consorting with people who are not of your own religion, make not friends of such men.'

When the Rabbi had finished his eloquent discourse his hearers were filled with joy and satisfaction. It is impossible to describe to you their happiness![281]

'Abdu'l-Bahá was saying that the main cause of misunderstanding and discord among nations is the misrepresentation of religion by the religious leaders. 'It is misguided ones like these who are the cause of division and hatred upon earth,' 'Abdu'l-Bahá said.

104

Hostile Towards One Another to the Bitter End

'The spiritual brotherhood which is enkindled and established through the breaths of the Holy Spirit unites nations and removes the cause of warfare and strife.'[282] 'Abdu'l-Bahá

A Muslim, a Christian and a Jew were rowing in a boat when all of a sudden the sea became very turbulent. The boat was tossed on the crest of the waves and the three riders saw that their lives were endangered.

The Muslim began praying, 'O God! Take the life of this Christian.'

The Christian prayed, 'O Father! Send to the bottom of the deep this Muslim.'

They noticed that the Jew was not offering any prayers. Therefore, they asked him, 'Why don't you pray for relief?'

He replied, 'I am praying – I am asking the Lord to answer the prayers of both of you.'[283]

The religion of God must create love and harmony amongst people and not hatred and discord.

105

The Thieves of Baghdad

'Seek not a single minute of rest and do not keep still. Travel more and more in cities and villages. Bear the glad-tidings and guide them. Strengthen the beloved and open the eye of perception of the strangers.'[284]   'Abdu'l-Bahá

Years ago in Baghdad the usual punishment for offenders and violators of the law was the bastinado. The governor noticed that a certain band of men came repeatedly before him for trial. They were regularly found guilty of breaking the law, sentenced, and whipped upon the feet. While the bastinado was being inflicted they appeared quite comfortable and unconscious of pain. In a few days these same offenders would be back again, going through the same process. The governor made careful inquiry about them. It was learned that they lived together in a house and that every day it was their custom to bastinado each other until the skin upon their feet had become so hardened to the whip that the legal bastinado gave them no inconvenience whatsoever.[285]

'Abdu'l-Bahá was telling the Bahá'ís that they must be united, that they must assist each other in their teaching work and that they must become impervious to criticism, attack and abuse.

106

This Kurd Often Forgot to Offer His Prayers

'Verily I am God and there is none other God but Me. Hence worship Me, and for the sake of Him Who is the Most Great Remembrance, offer ye prayers, purged from the insinuations of the people . . .'[286]   The Báb

A certain Kurd was awakened in the morning to say his prayers. He arose and prayed five times successively . . . The people said to him, 'What art thou doing? The morning prayer should be uttered only twice and thou art repeating it five times.' He replied, 'God bless you. I do not say my prayers often. When I do say them, why should I say them only twice? The more the better.'[287]

'Abdu'l-Bahá was commenting on His long journey to the West and His heavy schedule of activity in America after 40 years of imprisonment.

107

These Horses Run Long Distances at Great Speed

'Do not seek rest during night and day and sit not tranquil for a minute. Bring these glad-tidings to the hearing of mankind with the utmost exertion, and accept every calamity and affliction in your love for God and reliance on Abdul-Baha [sic].'[288]   'Abdu'l-Bahá

In Persia there is a wonderful breed of horses which are trained to run long distances at very great speed. They are most carefully trained at first. They are taken out into the fields and made to run a short course. At the commencement of their training they are not able to run far. The distance is gradually increased. They become thinner and thinner, wiry and lean, but their strength increases. Finally, after months of rigid training, their swiftness and endurance become wonderful. They are able to run at full speed across the rough country for many parasangs [parsangs].[289] At first this would have been impossible. Not until they become trained, thin and wiry, can they endure this severe test.[290]

After telling this story, 'Abdu'l-Bahá said, 'In this way I shall train you. "Kam-kam, kam-kam" (little by little, little by little), until your powers of endurance become so increased that you will serve the Cause of God continually, without other motive, without other thought or wish.'[291]

108

The Same Message Was Conveyed So Differently

'Endeavour to the utmost of thy powers to establish the word of truth with eloquence and wisdom and to dispel falsehood from the face of the earth.'[292]

Bahá'u'lláh

It is narrated that once Hárún ar-Rashíd dreamed that all his teeth had fallen out. A soothsayer was summoned. He interpreted the caliph's dream this way, 'All the children, grandchildren and relatives of the caliph will first die and then the caliph will die himself.'

Hárún ar-Rashíd became very sad and disturbed. He ordered the soothsayer to be imprisoned. Then he asked if there were any other soothsayers.

The answer was affirmative and another one was

brought to him. The caliph asked him to interpret the dream.

This soothsayer said, 'This dream indicates that his excellency the caliph will have a longer life than others.' Hárún ar-Rashíd became happy and amply rewarded the soothsayer.[293]

Teaching must be carried out with tact and in an agreeable manner.

109

She Kept Him Too Busy to Have Time to Divorce Her

'Say: Teach ye the Cause of God, O people of Bahá, for God hath prescribed unto every one the duty of proclaiming His Message, and regardeth it as the most meritorious of all deeds.'[294]
Bahá'u'lláh

[There was] a man whose wife had caused him such trouble and had kept him so busy that, when he was told to divorce her so as to get relief, he answered, 'She does not give me a chance to find time to give her a divorce.'[295]

'Abdu'l-Bahá was very tired from all the writing and speaking He had done. He jokingly told this story.

110

Napoleon Had More than a Map and a Few Needles

'Therefore, mere knowledge is not sufficient for complete human attainment. The teachings of the Holy Books need a heavenly power and divine potency to carry them out.'[296]
'Abdu'l-Bahá

Many years ago in Baghdád I saw a certain officer sitting upon the ground. Before him a large paper was placed into which he was sticking needles tipped with small red and white flags. First he would stick them into the paper, then thoughtfully pull them out and change their position. I watched him with curious interest for a long time, then asked, 'What are you doing?' He replied, 'I have in mind something which is historically related of Napoleon I during his war against Austria. One day, it is said, his secretary found him sitting upon the ground as I am now doing, sticking needles into a paper before him. His secretary inquired what it meant. Napoleon answered, "I am on the battlefield figuring out my next victory. You see, Italy and Austria are defeated, and France is triumphant." In the great campaign which followed, everything came out just as he said. His army carried his plans to a complete success. Now, I am doing the same as Napoleon, figuring out a great campaign of military conquest.' I said, 'Where is your army? Napoleon had an army already equipped when he figured out his victory. You have no army. Your forces exist only on paper. You have no power to conquer countries. First get ready your army, then sit upon the ground with your needles.'[297]

In His discourse, 'Abdu'l-Bahá said, 'Briefly, the teachings of the Holy Books need a divine potency to complete their accomplishment in human hearts.'[298]

III

Sincerity and Devotion Brought Them Recognition

'But one must show forth perseverance and self-devotion and consecrate his thoughts, until the tree of hope may give fruit and produce consequences.'[299]

'Abdu'l-Bahá

Núr 'Alí-Sháh[300] was rejected by both the government and the people. He became homeless and an exile. He could not live even in the holy shrines because of the transgressions of the religious authorities against him. At the end, he died in Baghdad.

A few of his servants, who were living in extreme poverty and adversity, were very sad on account of his calamities and homelessness. With much sincerity they began to commemorate his name. Since they did this with great sensitivity and devotion, each one of them became very famous, honourable and respected among all the people. Everyone was amazed at this. Even many of the ministers of the king and the members of the clergy became their close friends and devotees. All of this took place, despite the fact that their cause was not particularly important.[301]

'Abdu'l-Bahá was telling the friends that the work of teaching and serving the Faith must be carried out with sincerity of heart, spirituality and total attraction to His holy court.

112

She Wanted to be the First One to Throw a Grenade, So Did He

'The true lover yearneth for tribulation even as doth the rebel for forgiveness and the sinful for mercy.'[302]   Bahá'u'lláh

It was reported that two people, a girl and a boy, arrived in Moscow and entered a hotel. Their behaviour seemed strange to the hotel manager – they would not sleep, for example. The manager became suspicious and began to watch them. Then he informed the authorities. The two were searched and the papers which were found on them indicated that they had some disagreement with each other. One wanted to be the first to throw a grenade; the other also wanted to be the first one to do so. At any rate, it became clear to the authorities that both were against the government, wanted to establish democracy and were going to use grenades. The judgement was that they should be exiled to Siberia. As the two were being taken, they shouted: 'O people, we are sacrificing ourselves for you.'[303]

After relating this incident, 'Abdu'l-Bahá said, 'Now contemplate, if those who are concerned with the affairs of this world of dust are so proud, what should be the conduct of those who are devoted to the Lord of Eternity?'

113

Mullá Ḥasan Became a Bahá'í and an Enkindled Cook

'It behoveth every one in this Day of God to dedicate himself to the teaching of the Cause with utmost prudence and steadfastness.'[304]   Bahá'u'lláh

. . . in the city of Bagdad, I talked with a learned man, Mullah Hassan, some of whose relatives were believers. No matter how hard they tried to give him the Message, he would not accept it. Once, they brought him to my house when I was just getting up from my sleep and combing my hair. They said, 'We have brought so-and-so here and we beg you to come and speak with him; perhaps he will become a believer.' I said, 'Very well' and then I turned to the Blessed Beauty and prayed: 'O Blessed Beauty, confirm me!' Afterwards, I talked to him, and in the same hour he became a believer. He became exceedingly good and was so enkindled that, although he was of high rank, he used to go into the kitchen and cook things with his own hand to entertain the friends.[305]

'Abdu'l-Bahá was talking to the friends in Haifa about different topics including teaching the Faith.

114

This Man Became Susceptible and Accepted the Faith

'Only when the lamp of search, of earnest striving, of longing desire, of passionate devotion, of fervid love, of rapture, and ecstasy, is kindled within the seeker's heart, and the breeze of His loving-kindness is wafted upon his soul, will the darkness of error be dispelled, the mists of doubts and misgivings be dissipated, and the lights of knowledge and certitude envelop his being.'[306]

Bahá'u'lláh

When I was a child, there was a Bahá'í who had a non-Bahá'í brother. Whatever the Bahá'ís did or said, he would not accept the Faith. They brought him to me. He said, 'They have told me a lot about this Faith but up to now I have not been convinced.' I said to him, 'You are not susceptible enough. A thirsty person enjoys water and becomes satisfied. One who can see becomes content with seeing the sun or the moon but not a blind individual. A person who can hear enjoys a melodious song but not a deaf one. I talked to him much in this vein. He was transformed and accepted the Faith.[307]

'Abdu'l-Bahá was commenting on the attentiveness of a German boy who accompanied his parents to His meetings.

115

The King Loved Him and Therefore Tortured Him

'Thank thou God, thou art bearing trials in the path of the Kingdom and art enduring persecutions and sufferings. These afflictions are conducive to the spiritual development and the descent of the Holy Spirit.'[308]   'Abdu'l-Bahá

A certain ruler wished to appoint one of his subjects to a high office; so, in order to train him, the king cast him into prison and caused him to suffer much. The man was surprised at this, for he expected great favours. The ruler had him taken from the prison and beaten with sticks. This greatly astonished the man, for he thought the ruler loved him. After this he was hanged on the gallows until he was nearly dead. After he recovered he asked the ruler, 'If you love me, why did you do these things?' The ruler replied: 'I wish to make you prime minister. By having gone through these ordeals you are better fitted for that office. I wish you to know how it is yourself. When you are obliged to punish, you will know how it feels to endure these things. I love you so I wish you to become perfect.[309]

'Abdu'l-Bahá told this story to Mr Tinsley, whom He was visiting in hospital in San Francisco. 'Abdu'l-Bahá told him that he should not be sad and that his affliction would make him spiritually stronger.

116

Persecution of a Bábí Converted This Bystander

'They imagine that persecution and suffering will hinder the promulgation of the Cause; whereas no rampart is able to obstruct the descent of the waves of the Most Great Sea . . .'[310]   'Abdu'l-Bahá

[It is related] that the possessions of a certain Bábí in Káshán[311] were plundered, and his household scattered and dispersed. They stripped him naked and scourged him, defiled his beard, mounted him face backwards on an ass, and paraded him through the streets and bazaars with the utmost cruelty, to the sound of drums, trumpets, guitars, and tambourines. A certain *gabr* [Zoroastrian] who knew absolutely naught of the world or its denizens chanced to be seated apart in a corner of a caravansary. When the clamour of the people rose high he hastened into the street, and, becoming cognizant of the offence and the offender, and the cause of his public disgrace and punishment in full detail, he fell to making search, and that very day entered the society of the Bábís, saying, 'This very ill-usage and public humiliation is a proof of truth and the very best of arguments. Had it not been thus it might have been that a thousand years would have passed ere one like me became informed.'[312]

Just before relating this episode, 'Abdu'l-Bahá wrote, '. . . to interfere with matters of conscience is simply to give them greater currency and strength; the more you strive to extinguish the more will the flame be kindled . . .'[313]

117

Mu'tamid Received Eternal Life Because of His Fairness

'Well is it with that divine whose head is attired with the crown of justice, and whose temple is adorned with the ornament of equity.'[314]   Bahá'u'lláh

In the meeting of Mu'tamid,[315] the Báb was asked whether the Qur'án was an authority and a proof for those who were present at the time or was addressed to absent ones as well. He answered that absence and presence did not exist in the sight of God. The son of Kalbásí[316] said that his late father had not mentioned such a thing in his treatise. At this response and the inequities of other mullás in the face of Báb's convincing answer, the Mu'tamid was transformed and became a believer. Now perceive what an eternal life he received because of his fairness and what a death and loss came to them as the result of their cruelty and oppression.[317]

'Abdu'l-Bahá was talking about Mu'tamidu'd-Dawlih, mentioning that the memory of good and just individuals made Him very happy.

118

Banishment and Persecution Raised the Divine Flag

'Behold how in this Dispensation the worthless and foolish have fondly imagined that by such instruments as massacre, plunder and banishment they can extinguish the Lamp which the Hand of Divine power hath lit, or eclipse the Day Star of everlasting splendour.'[318] Bahá'u'lláh

It was a very cold winter. We arrived in Kirmán<u>sh</u>áh and were housed in an inn adjacent to a moat. It was all misery and affliction. Since it was for the sake of God, however, we were happy and in high spirits. In Asadábád[319] it was extremely cold, some 38 degrees below zero. My socks were wet and my feet were frostbitten. At night we planned to have halva but instead of sugar they had added pepper, which burned our mouths and throats. That night we could not sleep at all – we were drinking water all night long. The divine flag which is now flying high is the blessing of those pains and exiles.[320]

'Abdu'l-Bahá was welcoming a group of pilgrims and commenting on the hardships associated with travelling. Then He began to talk about the banishment of Bahá'u'lláh from Tehran to Iraq.

119

A Revolver Couldn't Scare This Olympian Camel

'Therefore, the people of darkness imagine that they can oppose (this Revelation); yet, ere long they shall find themselves in loss and consternation! They shall observe that the power of the Word of God hath subdued East and West.'[321] 'Abdu'l-Bahá

Mohammed Ali Pasha [Muḥammad 'Alí Páshá][322] had a big, fat camel. When the Hajis started on their long pilgrimage to Mecca through the desert, he ordered a rapid-fire gun to be mounted on the back of the camel and fired each time that they halted. The . . . camel was so accustomed to the thundering noise of the cannon, that although it was fired on its back, it never moved. Because this camel performed such an important service and carried such a heavy load, the Pasha had ordered that it could graze through anybody's farm without any hindrance. Having reached a station, the camel entered the farm of a poor farmer. In his absence he had left a young boy to drive away the animals. On seeing the camel the boy started to scare it away by firing in the air with a small revolver. 'What are you doing, my boy?' a Haji asked. 'I want to scare away this camel.' 'O, don't trouble yourself. On the back of this camel a cannon is fired twice daily, and it does not move. Do not expect to scare him away with the sound of a small revolver.'[323]

Opposition to the Faith cannot stop its onward march.

120

The Poor Farmer Watered His Parched Piece of Land

'O ye loved ones of God! Praise be to Him, the bright banner of the Covenant is flying higher every day, while the flag of perfidy hath been reversed, and hangeth at half-mast.'[324]
                                                                    'Abdu'l-Bahá

Once upon a time, there was a poor fellah (farmer) who cultivated a patch of ground with cotton. His neighbouring farmers were all rich landlords and Pashas, and so they prevented in a high-handed manner this poor farmer from receiving his just share of water wherewith to irrigate his parched farm. He appealed several times to their sense of justice, but they laughed him out of their presence. Finally, realizing that his cotton would dry and his labours fail of result, he went one midnight and changed the [course] of the stream toward his own farm, and irrigated it most thoroughly. When in the morning the landlords saw what their neighbour had done so daringly, they sent for him and rebuked him severely. Not being satisfied with this, they bastinadoed him very hard. While he was undergoing this cruel punishment, he cried out, 'O ye men! I have already irrigated my farm. This will do you no good. I have saved my crop from destruction by the drought! Why do you inflict upon me such a useless torture? The earth is watered!'[325]

'Abdu'l-Bahá told this story to the friends after He had built the Báb's Holy Tomb on Mount Carmel despite the opposition of the Covenant-breakers and the enemies of the Faith.

121

Since He Was Not Her Beloved She Punished Him

'Lord! Shield Thou from these Covenant-breakers the mighty Stronghold of Thy Faith and protect Thy secret Sanctuary from the onslaught of the ungodly.'[326]

'Abdu'l-Bahá

'Alawiyyih Khánum, the wife of the martyr Mullá 'Alí Ján-i-Shahíd, had a dream. She related it to Jamál-i-Burújirdí.[327] She told him that in her dream Jamál-i-Mubárak [the Blessed Beauty] had come to visit her and had blessed her. Jamál said, 'Your dream was a true one – I have come here and I like you.'[328] It would have been appropriate if she had done to Jamál what the princess did to that clumsy fellow. The princess had fallen in love with Mírzá 'Alí Khán-i-Núrí. One day she heard that a guest had arrived in the room. Thinking that the guest was none other than Mírzá 'Alí Khán-i-Núrí, she took a light and entered the room where she found a coarse and ugly man. She raised both hands and began hitting the man on the head until his hat fell apart. All the while she was screaming, 'Are you Mírzá 'Alí Khán-i-Núrí? Are you Mírzá 'Alí Khán-i-Núrí? You poor devil, are you Mírzá 'Alí Khán-i-Núrí?'[329]

'Abdu'l-Bahá was in good mood and wanted everybody to be happy, so He told this story.

122

The Skilled Barber Did Not Pass the Test

'I fear lest, bereft of the melody of the dove of heaven, ye will sink back to the shades of utter loss, and, never having gazed upon the beauty of the rose, return to water and clay.'[330]

Bahá'u'lláh

It is related that a man entered a mental hospital and saw a very polite individual sitting calmly on the floor. The visitor asked him, 'What are you doing here and why have they brought you?'

He answered, 'I had many enemies because I was a skilled barber and the caliph had total confidence in me. My enemies became jealous and accused me of insanity. They started this rumour and made an uproar. Eventually the caliph heard about it. They all conspired with each other and sent me to this place.'

To test him, the inquirer asked, 'How do you cut hair?'

He answered, 'First you fix the apron on the customer, then sharpen the razor, wet the hair, massage the head and finally cut the hair.'

The inquirer said, 'Very good; now tell me how you proceed with the letting of blood.'

The man answered, 'First I tie the tourniquet, massage the area over the vein until it becomes large, sharpen the blade and then I stab you in the belly.'

As he raised his hand to strike, the inquirer said, 'I understand very well – stop right there! Up to this point, you were doing all right; too bad that you could not continue in that fashion.'[331]

'Abdul-Bahá was talking about the Covenant-breaking activities of Mírzá Áqá Ján towards the end of his earthly life.

123

No One Could Afford to Buy This Cheap Camel

'These natural impurities are evil qualities: anger, lust, worldliness, pride, lying, hypocrisy, fraud, self-love, etc.'[332]

'Abdu'l-Bahá

One day a man became annoyed with his camel and promised himself that on the following day he would sell it for
one s͟háhí (a small monetary unit). This person was a religious man and was always faithful to his promises. The
following morning, however, he regretted his promise and
wondered what to do. After much thinking, he came up
with a trick to save his camel. He tied a cat to the camel's
neck and began advertising his camel for one s͟háhí. People
gathered around him and everyone wanted to buy the beast
for that price. He said, 'Yes, the price of the camel is one
s͟háhí but that of the cat is a thousand qurús͟h (a unit much
larger than a s͟háhí). Both must be sold together.'

People became disappointed and went away. After a
while a customer came to him and said, 'I have heard that
you are selling your camel for one s͟háhí.'

The owner replied, 'Yes, here it is; but you must also buy
the cat for a thousand qurús͟h.'

The customer, who liked the camel very much, said, 'I will
give you one hundred s͟háhí for the camel but you keep the cat.'

The owner of the camel said, 'That is not possible.'

Then the customer sighed a long sigh and said, 'The
camel would be one of a kind if that accursed cat were not
attached to his neck.'[333]

*'Abdu'l-Bahá's tranquillity and happiness in America were checked, at times,
by acts of treachery on the part of Dr Fareed, who was in His company.
Asked about His stay in Dublin, New Hampshire, 'Abdu'l-Bahá said that it
was fine but that it would have been better without Dr Fareed's presence. He
then related this story.*

124

He Supplicated with Much Sincerity

'Thus God instructeth whosoever seeketh Him. He, verily, loveth the one that

turneth towards Him. There is none other God but Him, the Forgiving, the Most Bountiful.'[334]   Bahá'u'lláh

There was . . . a Baktashi who, in his younger days, was an officer in the Turkish government. This man became very sick, and the members of his family had summoned a Mullah to his bed. Then [I] called on him and they asked the Mullah to pray that God might forgive his sins before his death. After the performance of some ceremonials, the Mullah, in his most solemn voice, told the patient to repeat the formula: 'Oh, God! I have sinned much. Confer upon me thy forgiveness.' The sick man did not answer. The Mullah repeated the formula over and over, but to no effect. Finally the patient, getting tired with this repetition, turned his eyes to the Mullah and said with earnestness: 'Man! for many years I have sinned against God and his servants. I have ransacked houses, orphaned children, burned hearts and committed all kinds of iniquities. Is the government of God so childlike as to forgive all my past sins by the repetition of a mere formula? Is God's system of dispensing justice so loose? Be gone, thou ignorant Mullah! Thou art telling me all these things to get ten Piasters as thy fee. Come, come, my friends, give him some money and let him depart quickly from my presence. He is a Satan and a tempter.' Then the Mullah left the room in haste, and when [I] was alone with him, the sick man fell on his knees and from the depths of his heart, cried out: 'Oh Lord! Oh Lord! I am a real sinner and Thou art the just God! I beg Thy Mercy! I have committed many sins. I have not done that which Thou hast commanded me and have practised those things which Thou hast made unlawful. With humility and contrition I am standing in Thy Presence. Do with me whatsoever Thou willest!' Abdul Baha was much affected by this outpouring of sincerity and departed, praying that his supplication might become accepted at the Threshold of the Almighty.[335]

We must supplicate and offer our prayers with sincerity and a pure heart.

125

A Sinner Who Depended Upon God Was Acceptable to Him

'When the sinner findeth himself wholly detached and freed from all save God, he should beg forgiveness and pardon from Him.'[336] Bahá'u'lláh

Once a Pharisee and a Publican entered the Temple to pray. The Pharisee said: 'Thank God I am not as other men.' The other said: 'God have mercy upon me, a sinner!' Christ said of these two: 'The Pharisee is not acceptable in the Kingdom of God, but the other is acceptable, because the Pharisee is trusting in his own action, but the other is depending upon the forgiveness of God.'[337]

'Abdu'l-Bahá remarked that God always loves those who repent and are sorry for what they have done. He added that the one who repents should remain firm in his repentance.

126

A Verse from the Qur'án Knocked <u>Gh</u>azalí Unconscious

'And when man attacheth his heart wholly to God and becometh related to the Blessed Perfection, the divine bounty will dawn.'[338] 'Abdu'l-Bahá

It is related that once Muḥammad <u>Gh</u>azalí[339] entered the Ádineh Mosque[340] where he heard someone reciting the verse, 'O my people who have been prodigal against yourselves, do not despair of God's mercy.'[341]

As soon as he heard this recitation he raised his voice and shouted, 'Glad tidings and great rejoicing; He has related us to Himself by saying, "O my people".' From sheer joy and happiness he swooned away and fell to the ground.[342]

'Abdu'l-Bahá ends the Tablet in which this story is related by saying that the friends must be extremely joyful for being addressed 'O servants of the Abhá Beauty' and should know that this is indeed a great honour for them.

127

Since He Accepted the Will of God as His Own, He Was Happy

'The source of all good is trust in God, submission unto His command, and contentment with His holy will and pleasure.'[343]   Bahá'u'lláh

A man asked another: 'In what station are you?' The other answered: 'In the utmost happiness.' 'Where does this happiness come from?' 'Because all existing things move according to my wish . . . Therefore I have no sorrow. There is no doubt that all the beings move by the Will of God, and I have given up my own will, desiring the Will of God. Thus my will became the Will of God, for there is nothing of myself. All are moving by His Will, yet they are moving by my own will. In this case I am very happy.'[344]

'Abdu'l-Bahá added, 'When man surrenders himself, everything will move according to his wish.'

128

To Preserve His System the King Left His Kingdom

'One of Bahá'u'lláh's teachings is the adjustment of means of livelihood in human society. Under this adjustment there can be no extremes in human conditions as regards wealth and sustenance.'[345]   'Abdu'l-Bahá

The poor and the rich, according their degrees, can live happily, with ease and tranquillity. The first person in the world who had this idea was the king of Sparta. He sacrificed his kingdom for this work. He lived before Alexander the Great was born. This thought came to his mind, that he could render a service which would be higher than all services and become the cause of happiness to many. Thus he divided the people of Sparta into three divisions. One division consisted of the ancient inhabitants, and they were the farmers. Another division consisted of the industrial people; another were the Greeks, who were originally from Phoenicia. The name of this king was Lycurgus. He desired real equality among these three divisions, and in this manner established a just government. He said that the ancient people, who were the farmers, were free from any obligation except that they had to pay one-tenth of their products and no more. The people of industry and commerce had to pay yearly taxes and nothing else. The third class, who were the nobles and descendants of the rulers, whose occupations were in politics, war and the defence of the country, had all the land of Sparta. He measured the whole land and divided it equally among them. For example, there were nine thousand of them. He divided all the land in nine thousand equal parts and gave one part to each one of them. He gave one-tenth of the product of each piece of land to the one who owned it. He also made other laws and ordinances for the citizens. When he found that he had accomplished what he wanted, he said: 'I am going to Syria, but I am afraid that after I go away you will change my laws. Therefore, take an oath that you will not make any change before my return.' They took an oath in the temple and assured him that they would never make any change and that they would maintain these laws always until the return of the king. But the king left the temple, travelled and never returned. He gave up his kingdom in order that these laws might be preserved. This equality of distribution, in a short time, became the cause of discord, because one of these men had five children, another three children, and another two children. Differences accrued and the whole thing was upset. Therefore the matter of equality is an impossibility.[346]

The subject of 'Abdu'l-Bahá's discourse here is the spiritual solution to economic problems, one of Bahá'u'lláh's principles.

129

Zenobia Refused to Become the Empress of Rome

'The world of humanity has two wings – one is women and the other men. Not until both wings are equally developed can the bird fly.'[347]

'Abdu'l-Bahá

In past ages noted women have arisen in the affairs of nations and surpassed men in their accomplishments. Among them was Zenobia, Queen of the East, whose capital was Palmyra. Even today the site of that city bears witness to her greatness, ability and sovereignty; for there the traveller will find ruins of palaces and fortifications of the utmost strength and solidity built by this remarkable woman in the third century after Christ. She was the wife of the governor-general of Athens. After her husband's death she assumed control of the government in his stead and ruled her province most efficiently. Afterward she conquered Syria, subdued Egypt and founded a most wonderful kingdom with political sagacity and thoroughness. The Roman Empire sent a great army against her. When this army, replete with martial splendour reached Syria, Zenobia herself appeared upon the field leading her forces. On the day of battle she arrayed herself in regal garments, placed a crown upon her head and rode forth, sword in hand, to meet the invading legions. By her courage and military strategy the Roman army was routed and so completely dispersed that they were not able to reorganize in retreat. The government of Rome held consultation, saying, 'No matter what commander we send, we cannot overcome her; therefore, the Emperor Aurelian himself must go to lead the legions of Rome against Zenobia.' Aurelian marched into Syria with two hundred thousand soldiers. The army of Zenobia was greatly inferior in size. The Romans besieged her in Palmyra two years without success. Finally, Aurelian was able to cut off the city's supply of provisions so that she and her people were compelled by starvation to surrender. She was not defeated in battle. Aurelian carried her captive to Rome. On the day of his entry into the city he arranged a triumphal procession – first elephants, then lions, tigers, birds, monkeys – and after the monkeys, Zenobia. A crown was upon her head, a chain of gold about her neck. With queenly dignity and unconscious of humiliation, looking to the right and left, she said, 'Verily, I glory in being a woman and in having withstood the Roman Empire.' (At that time the dominion of Rome covered half the known earth.) 'And this chain about my neck is a sign not of humiliation but of glorification. This is a symbol of my power, not of my defeat.'[348]

'Abdu'l-Bahá was talking about some of the great and famous women of the world.

130

Catherine, the Clever Empress of Russia

'When all mankind shall receive the same opportunity of education and the equality of men and women be realized, the foundations of war will be utterly destroyed.'[349]
'Abdu'l-Bahá

Among other historical women was the wife of Peter the Great (Catherine I). Russia and Turkey were at war. The commander of the Turkish forces, Mohammed Pasha, defeated Peter at Servia [Serbia] and was about to take St Petersburgh [sic]. The Russians were in a most critical position. Catherine the wife of Peter the Great said, 'I will arrange this matter.' She had an interview with Mohammad Pasha, negotiated a treaty of peace and induced him to turn back. She saved her husband and her nation. This was a great accomplishment. Afterward she was crowned and governed with the utmost ability.[350]

Equality of men and women was the subject of 'Abdu'l-Bahá's talk.

131

The Erudite and Courageous Ṭáhirih

'History records the appearance in the world of women who have been signs of guidance, power and accomplishment.'[351]
'Abdu'l-Bahá

Qurratu'l-'Ayn (Ṭáhirih) was eloquent. Her writings and poems are available today. Every one of the learned of the region praised her. She had such an authority and force of presence that in all her debates she always prevailed over the religious doctors. They lacked the courage to enter into a contest with her. Since she was the promoter of the Bábí

Faith, the government imprisoned and persecuted her but she never became silent.

In prison she would cry out and guide the people. Eventually they condemned her to death. She was courageous, however, and was never overtaken by lassitude. She was imprisoned in the house of the mayor of the city. It so happened that there was a wedding in that house and hence all means of pleasure, gaiety, music, singing, eating and drinking were available.

Qurratu'l-'Ayn began to speak in such a way that everyone left the delights and pleasures of the occasion and gathered around her. No one paid any attention to the wedding. All were amazed by her and she was the sole speaker.

When the king ordered her to be killed she dressed and adorned herself with the utmost care, although it was not her custom to be concerned with her appearance. People were surprised and asked her, 'What are you doing?'

She replied, 'It is my wedding day.' With much dignity and quiescence she went to the garden (her place of martyrdom). Everyone was saying that she was going to be killed but she continued her address, saying, 'I am the sound of the bugle mentioned in the Gospels.'

Then they killed her and threw her body into a well.[352]

'Abdu'l-Bahá was talking about the famous and influential women in the world.

132

Vaḥíd Received a Profound Lecturing from Ṭáhirih

'Guidance hath ever been given by words, and now it is given by deeds. Every one must show forth deeds that are pure and holy, for words are the property of all alike, whereas such deeds as these belong only to Our loved ones.'[353]

Bahá'u'lláh

One day the great Siyyid Yaḥyá, surnamed Vaḥíd, was present there [house of Bahá'u'lláh]. As he sat without, Ṭáhirih
listened to him from behind a curtain. I was then a child,
and was sitting on her lap. With eloquence and fervour,
Vaḥíd was discoursing on the signs and verses that bore witness to the advent of the new Manifestation. She suddenly
interrupted him and, raising her voice, vehemently
declared: 'O Yaḥyá! Let deeds, not words, testify to thy
faith, if thou art a man of true learning. Cease idly repeating the traditions of the past, for the day of service, of
steadfast action, is come. Now is the time to show forth the
true signs of God, to rend asunder the veils of idle fancy, to
promote the Word of God, and to sacrifice ourselves in His
path. Let deeds, not words, be our adorning!'[354]

This is part of 'Abdu'l-Bahá's account of the life of Ṭáhirih.

133

Vaḥíd Showed His Great Humility and Devotion

*'Make me as dust in the pathway of Thy loved ones, and grant that I may
offer up my soul for the earth ennobled by the footsteps of Thy chosen ones in
Thy path, O Lord of Glory in the Highest.'*[355]   'Abdu'l-Bahá

I remember, when I was small, I was sitting one day in the
yard next to Siyyid Yaḥyá, Vaḥíd.[356] I saw Mírzá 'Alí
Sayyáḥ[357] clad in the attire of a dervish, but with bare feet,
arrive at the house. His feet were covered with mud.
Someone asked him where he was coming from. He said,
'From the castle of Máh-Kú and from the presence of His
Holiness the Báb.'
    Immediately, Vaḥíd threw himself on the feet of Sayyáḥ
and began to cry and to rub his beard on the muddy feet.
Notwithstanding his great fame and exalted position, Vaḥíd

did this because Sayyáḥ had come from the Beloved's abode. To such a degree he would show humility to the servants of the divine threshold.[358]

While travelling to California by train, 'Abdu'l-Bahá was talking to those in His company about the spiritual training provided by the Faith and its influence on people.

134

His Adobe Brick Outlasted All His Other Possessions

'Abandon not for that which perisheth an everlasting dominion, and cast not away celestial sovereignty for a worldly desire.'[359]   Bahá'u'lláh

Muʻtamidu'd-Dawlih of Isfahan, Manúchihr Khán, owned many buildings. He had many villages in the vicinity of Tehran. All these constructions, edifices and properties passed away. All were demolished – not a trace of them remains. But he installed a single adobe brick in the city of God. That brick remains; it was not destroyed. Privately, he protected the Báb from His enemies for a few days. Outwardly, he first expelled Him and then he safeguarded Him in the privacy of his own residence. He installed, in the city of God, this brick which will last forever. His impression will remain for eternity in the divine edifice.[360]

'Abdu'l-Bahá was talking about the virtues and nobility of Muʻtamidu'd-Dawlih.

135

He Prayed with Rapture

'The state of prayer is the best of conditions, for man is then associating with God.'[361]   'Abdu'l-Bahá

The late Pidar-Ján was among those believers who emigrated to Baghdád. He was a godly old man, enamoured of the Well-Beloved; in the garden of Divine love, he was like a rose full-blown. He arrived there, in Baghdád, and spent his days and nights communing with God and chanting prayers; and although he walked the earth, he travelled the heights of Heaven.

To obey the law of God, he took up a trade, for he had nothing. He would bundle a few pairs of socks under his arm and peddle them as he wandered through the streets and bázárs, and thieves would rob him of his merchandise. Finally he was obliged to lay the socks across his outstretched palms as he went along. But he would get to chanting a prayer, and one day he was surprised to find that they had stolen the socks, laid out on his two hands, from before his eyes. His awareness of this world was clouded, for he journeyed through another. He dwelt in ecstasy; he was a man drunken, bedazzled.

For some time, that is how he lived in 'Iráq. Almost daily he was admitted to the presence of Bahá'u'lláh. His name was 'Abdu'lláh but the friends bestowed on him the title of Pidar-Ján – Father Dear – for he was a loving father to them all. At last, under the sheltering care of Bahá'u'lláh, he took flight to the 'seat of truth, in the presence of the potent king'.[362]

This is part of 'Abdu'l-Bahá's account of the life of this saintly believer.

136

He Was Disowned by His Father Yet He Inherited All

'Thou dost bestow wealth upon whomsoever Thou willest and dost reduce to poverty whomsoever Thou willest. Thou dost cause whomsoever Thou willest to prevail over whomsoever Thou willest.'[363]   The Báb

When the Blessed Beauty was residing in Baghdad, there was a Shí'í Muslim by the name of Shaykh 'Abdu'l-Hamíd who had a tremendous love and affection for Bahá'u'lláh. At the time of His departure from Baghdad, this man ran a distance of ten miles, escorting Bahá'u'lláh out of the city.

Sometime later, however, all his love and affection changed to anger and enmity. This happened because one of the friends arranged for a big celebration during the festival of Riḍván, which had coincided with Áshúrá,[364] and he had openly demonstrated his joy and happiness. This incident made the Shí'í community extremely angry and caused Shaykh 'Abdu'l-Hamíd to become such an enemy that, with a gun in hand, he went to the blessed house in the middle of the night to kill all the people who lived there.

But one of the sons of this Shaykh became a believer. All the pleas and insistence of the father failed to make his son, Shaykh Muḥammad, leave the Faith. To force his son to abandon his belief, Shaykh 'Abdu'l-Hamíd eventually bequeathed all his possessions to his other sons and deprived Shaykh Muḥammad of his wealth. To make it impossible for Shaykh Muḥammad to appeal to the courts after the father's death, Shaykh 'Abdu'l-Hamíd officially sold all his properties to his other sons and registered the receipt of the money in the Ottoman court and in the consulate.

Thereafter, Shaykh Muḥammad became poor. With great difficulty, and on foot, he came to 'Akká. He visited the Blessed Beauty, who sent him to Iran to teach. In Iran he travelled extensively, met the Bahá'ís and achieved great results.

Now you see how God works. First <u>Sh</u>ay<u>kh</u> Muḥammad's brothers and then his father died, one by one. The court in Baghdad wrote to Iran asking <u>Sh</u>ay<u>kh</u> Muḥammad to come to that city because all the belongings of his brothers and his father were there waiting for him. He went to Baghdad and took possession of everything.[365]

'Abdu'l-Bahá was talking to His audience about past events.

137

One Bahá'í Sacrificed Himself for Another

'The fundamental purpose animating the Faith of God and His Religion is to safeguard the interests and promote the unity of the human race, and to foster the spirit of love and fellowship amongst men.'[366]   Bahá'u'lláh

Sydney Sprague[367] had fallen a victim to cholera in Punjab. When the Bahá'ís in Bombay heard of this, one of them named Kay<u>kh</u>usraw, with no thought of himself, rushed north to nurse him and was by his bedside day and night. Sprague recovered. Kay<u>kh</u>usraw contracted cholera and died.[368]

'Abdu'l-Bahá was speaking at a dinner party and said of Kay<u>kh</u>usraw, a Bahá'í of Parsi origin, 'He was the first Oriental friend to give his life for a Western Bahá'í brother.' He bestowed upon him the station of a martyr.

138

His Bad Answers Were Due to His Misunderstanding

'Among the things which are conducive to unity and concord and will cause the whole earth to be regarded as one country is that the divers languages be reduced to one language and in like manner the scripts used in the world be confined to a single script.'[369]   Bahá'u'lláh

There were once two friends who did not know each other's language. One fell ill and the other went to see him.

Using signs and gestures the visitor asked his friend how he was.

The sick man answered that he was about to die.

His friend misunderstood and thought that he was saying he was better. Therefore, he replied, 'God be praised.'

Again, using a sign or two, the visitor asked, 'What have you taken?'

The friend said, 'Poison.'

The visitor said, 'May it bring you a speedy recovery.'

Then the visitor asked, 'Who is your doctor?'

The sick friend replied, "Izrá'íl (the angel of death).'

The visitor responded by saying, 'May his presence restore your health.'

A third person, who was a witness to this conversation, informed the visitor of his inappropriate answers.

The visitor said, 'I thought that my friend's answers to the questions were: 'I am better, I took this medicine and my doctor is such and such a person.' Therefore, my responses were: 'God be praised, may it bring you a speedy recovery and may his presence restore your health.'[370]

With a universal auxiliary language all will be able to communicate with one another with ease.

139

Four Travellers Quarrelled Over the Same Fruit

'The day is approaching when all the peoples of the world will have adopted one universal language and one common script. When this is achieved, to whatsoever city a man may journey, it shall be as if he were entering his own home.'[371]   Bahá'u'lláh

At the city gate sat four travellers, a Persian, a Turk, an Arab and a Greek. They were hungry and wanted their evening meal. So one was selected to buy for them all. But among them they could not agree as to what should be bought. The Persian said angoor, the Turk uzum, the Arab wanted aneb and the Greek clamoured for staphylion green and black. They quarrelled and wrangled and almost came to blows in trying to prove that the particular desire of each was the right food. When all of a sudden there passed a donkey ladened with grapes. Each man sprang to his feet and with eager hands pointed out: 'See uzum!' said the Turk. 'See aneb!' said the Arab. 'See angoor!' said the Persian. And the Greek said, 'See, staphylion!' Then they bought their grapes and were at peace.[372]

The story emphasizes the need for a common language.

140

The Members of This Club Were Clever but Silent

'And among the teachings of Bahá'u'lláh is the origination of one language that may be spread universally among the people. This teaching was revealed from the pen of Bahá'u'lláh in order that this universal language may eliminate misunderstandings from among mankind.'[373]   'Abdu'l-Bahá

There was once organized in Persia a society whose chief characteristic was that they spoke without the tongue, and with the slightest sign could communicate many important matters. This society progressed to such a degree that with the motion of a finger abstruse matters could be understood. The government feared that they might organize a society against the government and since none could understand their purpose they might work great mischief. Therefore they suppressed them.

I wish to tell you a story about this society. Anyone who desired to join it had to stand at the door. Then they consulted with each other by signs and gave their opinions without speaking. Once a person with an awful looking visage stood at the door. The president looked at his face and saw what an awful looking figure he had. There was a cup on the table containing water. The president poured in some water until it was full to the brim. This was the sign of rejection. It meant that there was no room among them for that person. But the man was intelligent. He took a tiny piece of flower leaf and with the utmost deference entered the room and put it on the surface of the water in the cup. He laid it so carefully that the water in the cup did not move. All were delighted. He meant that he did not need a big place, that he was like a flower leaf which does not need [space]. They clapped their hands and accepted him.[374]

A visitor told 'Abdu'l-Bahá that he was sorry he did not know Persian. 'Abdu'l-Bahá said, 'Praise be to God, this veil does not exist in the world of the spirit. The hearts speak with each other.'[375] Then He told this story.

141

The Turk Thought He Was Being Insulted

'. . . and the greatest means for the promotion of that unity is for the peoples of the world to understand one another's writing and speech.'[376] Bahá'u'lláh

A Turk came here [the Holy Land] and one of the inhabitants told him, 'You are the *light* of my eye.' This he said in the utmost love. The Arabs use this expression to convey the utmost love. In Turkish it ['*ayn*] means a bear. So this man picked him up and threw him on the ground. One who knew the language came and said, 'What are you doing?' He replied, 'This man calls me a bear.' The other avowed, 'By God, I said the *light* of my eye.'[377]

'Abdu'l-Bahá was talking with the friends about the benefits of a universal language. He said, 'In the same way that the language of the Kingdom is one, so also should the human tongues be one.'

142

In This Contest the Greeks Just Polished the Wall

'Cleanse thy heart with the burnish of the spirit, and hasten to the court of the Most High.'[378]   Bahá'u'lláh

[At some period of history, there was a rivalry between Greek and Japanese artists.] This competition became so keen that an opportunity was given to these artists to compare their skill. A gallery was provided and the rivals were to decorate opposite sides. A sliding scaffolding concealed the work of one party from the other. Finally, the day of the test came. The king and his party inspected first the work of the Japanese, who had most wonderfully depicted figures, scenes and objects on their side of the wall, in a manner which was superlatively great. When the other side was unveiled it [transpired] that the Greeks had devoted their time to polishing their side, and it was so perfectly done that the pictures from the opposite side were mirrored therein and depicted even more exquisitely.[379]

We must polish the mirror of our heart and try to become more spiritual, was 'Abdu'l-Bahá's advice.

143

A Suitable and Touching Song Would Persuade the King

'In this dispensation, music is one of the arts that is highly approved and is considered to be the cause of the exaltation of sad and desponding hearts.'[380]
'Abdu'l-Bahá

Among the most ancient musicians of Persia was one named Barbad. When a great question was asked at the court of the king and the ministers failed in persuading the king, the matter would be referred to Barbad. Whereupon Barbad would go with his instrument to the court and would play the most appropriate and touching music: and the end would at once be gained. Because the king would immediately be affected by the musical melodies. Certain feelings of generosity would swell in his heart, and he would give way.[381]

'Abdu'l-Bahá commented that if the utterances of God are melodiously chanted, they will be most impressive.

144

The Ministers Held Useful Meetings

'That one indeed is a man who, today, dedicateth himself to the service of the entire human race. The Great Being saith: Blessed and happy is he that ariseth to promote the best interests of the peoples and kindreds of the earth.'[382]
Bahá'u'lláh

The ministers of Fath-'Alí Sháh used to gather every night in a place and would arrange for a feast of friendship and sociability. They had chosen nights because they were calm and free from all the noise and fuss of the day. No one but the ministers themselves could attend these meetings. Even the serving attendants were excluded. In peace, happiness and unity they would discuss important issues and consult about them. Each topic was discussed and debated for one entire night or longer. When they reached a conclusion about which everyone felt quite certain, they would commit it to writing.

After this there remained no doubts or obstacles. They would accept neither intermediation nor defection. In this way, they would continue their deliberations and consultation until midnight.

Shortly before morning they would have their dinner and then would go their separate ways. During the following day they would enforce all that was decided and recorded. They had very pleasant and useful gatherings; not noisy and tumultuous ones.[383]

'Abdu'l-Bahá was giving some historical facts to visiting dignitaries.

145

This Prime Minister Used Wisdom and Diplomacy

'Above all else, the greatest gift and the most wondrous blessing hath ever been and will continue to be Wisdom. It is man's unfailing Protector. It aideth him and strengtheneth him.'[384]

Bahá'u'lláh

In one of its wars with Russia, Iran was defeated. Seventy-six Russians were commissioned to handle the details of disengagement and the repatriation of the prisoners of war. Among the Russian prisoners was a woman who had married an Iranian, and they had two children. Whatever the Russians did in order to persuade her husband to bring her to them was of no avail. Eventually they went after her themselves. They were informed that she was in a public bathing house. After she left the bath, the Russians put her on a horse and took her with them. This caused a great commotion and uproar in which all the Russians were killed.

This development created a big problem for Iran. The prime minister said that he would settle the conflict peacefully. Then he wrote a long letter to St Petersburg. In it he elaborated on the issue of chastity and the extreme importance that the Iranians attach to it.

He wrote, 'On this subject, the Iranians have been blinded with fanaticism and bigotry. We are extremely sorry, nay ashamed, over this incident. If we have to retaliate, the killing of a few despicable individuals and rabble would hardly provide a befitting ransom. Instead, we are sending to you a venerable prince who is very dear to us. By taking the life of such an honourable individual, you will be absolving us from this sorrow and shame.'

The king of Russia took a liking to the prince after his arrival in that country. The king said to him, 'You are my son.' He did nothing to the prince except show him much kindness.[385]

Speaking on the subject of the ongoing war at that time, 'Abdu'l-Bahá was mentioning the importance of diplomacy and wisdom in dealing with conflicts.

146

With Two More Drinks He Would Have Become God

'The integrity of every rank and station must needs be preserved. By this is meant that every created thing should be viewed in the light of the station it hath been ordained to occupy.'[386]   Bahá'u'lláh

It is said that at one time a king went out travelling incognito. He put on a humble suit of clothes and started on his way in a scorching desert and finally reached the door of an Arab tent. The Arab finding the man exhausted from heat and hunger dragged him under the shade. When the king was revived he asked the Arab what he had to eat and drink. 'I have a goat skin of wine and a little goat,' the Arab answered. 'Very well, bring the wine and kill the goat to be cooked,' he said. The wine was brought. When the king drank one cup of wine he looked at the Arab and said: 'Do you know who I am?' 'No.' 'Then you must know that I am a soldier in the king's army.' The Arab was glad to entertain a brave man. The king drank another cup of wine. 'Do you know who I am?' 'Who are you?' 'I am a minister in the king's council chamber.' 'I am delighted to receive such a distinguished statesman.' A third cup was taken. 'Do you know who I am?' 'Well!' 'I am the king himself.' The Arab could not stand it any longer. He arose and took the goat-skin of wine from him. 'Why do you do this?' the guest asked astonished. 'Because I believe if you drank another cup you would be the Prophet of God, and a fifth cup would raise you to the station of God, so it is better for you to stop.'[387]

Some people become proud because of their outward circumstances, such as wealth and position.

147

Satan Woke Him Up to Say His Prayers with Vanity

'This lower nature in man is symbolized as Satan – the evil ego within us, not an evil personality outside.'[388]   'Abdu'l-Bahá

. . . one day Satan went to the bedside of Mu'áwiyah[389] and woke him up to perform his obligatory prayer. Mu'áwiyah said, 'O Satan, you never do any good or charitable work. Tell me your real purpose in waking me up.'

Satan said, 'The truth is this, you lead the congregational prayer with much pride, vanity and selfishness. Leading the prayer in this way is a greater sin and entails more deprivation than failing to offer your prayer altogether. For this reason I woke you up. Otherwise, as you said, I do not perform benevolent acts.'[390]

The discussion with the pilgrims was about the political parties in Iran and their activities. 'Abdu'l-Bahá said that whatever they did was for their own benefit only.

148

Was Iram Really Built by This Mythical King?

'The meaning is that every individual member of humankind is exhorted and

commanded to set aside superstitious beliefs, traditions and blind imitation of ancestral forms in religion and investigate reality for himself.'[391]

'Abdu'l-Bahá

During the reign of Mu'áwiyah, the caliph, there was an Israelite who claimed to be a Muslim. He always had a ready answer for any question related to any subject – history, traditions, commentaries, etc. Once he was asked about the meaning of 'Iram with lofty pillars', which is recorded in the Qur'án.[392]

He answered, 'This was a garden, opposite the promised heaven, which was built by Shaddád[393] on earth. Its trees, leaves and flowers were of emerald, its blossoms of gems, its sands of pearls, its walls of gold and silver and its servants and maids thus and so. When its construction was complete, Shaddád wanted to enter it.

As he was dismounting his horse, with one foot still in the stirrup, 'Izra'íl, the angel of death, was commissioned to take his life.

As soon as the Muslims heard this incredible story, they included it in their commentaries.[394]

'Abdu'l-Bahá was talking to his audience about superstitions and traditional beliefs in Islam.

149

Following God's Example!

'That seeker should, also, regard backbiting as grievous error, and keep himself aloof from its dominion, inasmuch as backbiting quencheth the light of the heart, and extinguisheth the life of the soul.'[395]

Bahá'u'lláh

There was a man by the name of Maḥmúd who used to

speak ill of people. Once the Blessed Beauty advised him to refrain from gossiping.

He said, 'I am following the example of God. As God has repeatedly mentioned Adam's transgression in all the heavenly books, I am doing the same to other people.'

The Blessed Beauty smiled at this response.[396]

One must not defile one's tongue with backbiting.

150

The Jailer Thought that His Cruelty was Jihád

'O Oppressors on Earth! Withdraw your hands from tyranny, for I have pledged Myself not to forgive any man's injustice.'[397]   Bahá'u'lláh

Once there were some 50 Christians imprisoned in 'Akká. The jailer routinely beat and tortured them, thinking this to be a commendable deed and a service in the path of God. Through the persecution and torture he would extract money from them. If they refused to pay, he would beat them more and say that it was *jihád* (holy war).

At last, one of them informed me. I said to the authorities, 'These people, whether Christians or not, are not deserving of such cruelty. If anyone wants to wage holy war, he should go to the battleground [of the Russo-Turkish war] and fight the Russians. Why this tyranny?'

The government decreed that the jailer should receive 50 lashes.

Before long, his situation became so bad that he came to me and said that his family was in need of bread. Eventu-ally, he became a beggar.[398]

'Abdu'l-Bahá was talking to His listeners about some past events.

151

He Turned the Other Cheek for Another Slap

'Beware, beware that any soul take revenge or retaliate over another even if he be a bloodthirsty enemy. Beware, beware that any one rebuke or reproach a soul, though he may be an ill-wisher and an ill-doer.'[399]   'Abdu'l-Bahá

Once a person met his friend in the street, and after the exchange of courtesies, gave him a hard blow in the face. 'Why dost thou do this?' 'Hast thou not read in the Gospel wherein Christ says – Whosoever shall smite thee on thy right cheek, turn to him the other also! – Now according to this admonition, let me smite thee on thy left cheek also.' The man submitted to the second blow quite willingly, and they parted. Next day, they met each other again, and the man received two more blows on his cheeks without any evident murmur. They met the third day, and he was going to inflict upon him the same blows. 'Wait a minute, my friend. I am not the only person in the world to live according to the Teaching of Christ. Thou also art one. I have obeyed Him two days, and the next two days will be thy turn.' With these words, he smote the man on his cheek, and asked him to 'turn the other also'.[400]

In answering a question about disarmament, 'Abdu'l-Bahá made the statement, '. . . disarmament must be put into practice by all the nations and not only by one or two.'[401] *Then He told this story.*

152

The Guard's Only Concern Was His Own Sleep

'What mankind needeth in this day is obedience unto them that are in authority, and a faithful adherence to the cord of wisdom.'[402]   Bahá'u'lláh

During the war against a foreign nation one of the soldiers was stricken with a severe sickness. The military doctor, observing his case, recommended him to the sentry. 'Do as I tell you,' he said. 'This man will not sleep tonight. It is the crucial night of his sickness, but tomorrow morning he will feel much better. Nurse him very carefully and watch over him all night.' The doctor went and after sunset the sentry came around to take his position. After an hour or two, he saw the sick man was getting worse, bemoaning and lamenting loudly. In order to alleviate his pain, he gave him an opium pill. As a result of this, he slept soundly all night. In the morning the doctor came and saw that the condition of the patient was worse than the day before. Not being able to explain this relapse, he sent for the sentry. 'What did you give him last night?' 'Oh! he was so frantic with pain that I gave him only a pill of opium, after which he slept quietly, all night.' 'Did you think that I, a doctor, didn't know this remedy just as well, but I did not give it to him because it would have made him worse?' 'What could I do? On my watch-night I wanted to sleep, and this patient disturbed my sleep. I gave him an opium pill and it served its purpose. Tonight there will be another watchman. If the patient is getting worse, it does not trouble me in the least.'[403]

Obedience is a praiseworthy quality in man.

153

He Would Dance on the Roof with Sheer Joy

'Knowledge is one of the greatest benefits of God. To acquire knowledge is incumbent on all.'[404]
                                                                Bahá'u'lláh

It is reported that Khájih Naṣíru'd-Dín-i-Ṭúsí,[405] the great mathematician, would climb onto the roof of his house some nights to observe the movements of the celestial bodies. In this way he would try to solve astronomical problems. Whenever he resolved a difficult problem, he would get up and start dancing from sheer joy and excitement.

On these occasions he would say, 'The kings should come and see the cause of real happiness! They should come and learn about the essence of real joy.'[406]

'Abdu'l-Bahá was speaking to His listeners about the importance of the acquisition of arts and sciences as enjoined by Bahá'u'lláh.

154

The Conceited Theologian Could Not Swim

'Knowledge is as wings to man's life, and a ladder for his ascent. Its acquisition is incumbent upon everyone. The knowledge of such sciences, however, should be acquired as can profit the peoples of the earth, and not those which begin with words and end with words.'[407]   Bahá'u'lláh

Once there was a theologian who took a sea trip. While he was walking on the deck and watching the calm sea, the captain passed by and enquired about his health. Our friend was so full of his theology that he asked the captain, 'Do you know theology?' He answered: 'No.' 'Then', our student declared with much pompous dignity, 'half of your life is lost.' The captain did not answer him, but continued his walk. Another day the sea became very stormy and the ship was in danger of being wrecked. The captain called on the theologian and found him prostrated with sickness. 'Do you know how to swim?' he asked. 'No.' 'Then, all your life is lost,' the captain roared at him.[408]

Conceit and egotism are unworthy qualities in a human being.

155

He Was Half Naked and Skinny but Had a Mighty Support

'Hasten, O people, unto the shelter of God, in order that He may protect you from the heat of the Day whereon none shall find for himself any refuge or shelter except beneath the shelter of His Name, the clement, the forgiving!'[409]

Bahá'u'lláh

When we were in Baghdad we went hunting with a few of our friends. A dark and thinly clad Arab riding on a camel came close to us. One of the friends wanted to jokingly threaten him with a gun. Another friend stopped this action. The Arab wanted bread, tobacco, a pipe and fire flint. We gave him all that. He also wanted coffee, which we did not have. Content, he left at last. Then the man who had stopped the threatening said, 'We should not judge the fellow by his half-nakedness and his dark skinny body. He has many kinfolk and riders. If someone troubles him, he raises a cry and starts a big uproar. The riders rush to his help and the ones on foot come from behind and take revenge.'[410]

'Abdu'l-Bahá added, 'Our condition now is like that of the dark-skinned Bedouin. Outwardly we are naked, helpless, friendless and alone. But in reality the army of the Kingdom on High is our helper.'

156

It Was Chilly and He Did Not Want to Catch Cold

'The steed of this Valley [Search] is patience; without patience the wayfarer on this journey will reach nowhere and attain no goal.'[411]

Bahá'u'lláh

There was a poor man who had no cover for his head. For three years he went around bare-headed under all weather conditions: cold or hot, rain or sunshine. Eventually, a generous and good-hearted man felt pity for him and decided to provide him with a turban. He took the poor fellow to a fabric shop and ordered a piece of cloth for his head.

As soon as the draper began to measure the cloth, the poor man took hold of the end of the cloth and began rapidly wrapping it around his head. The draper said to him, 'Wait until I measure the piece and cut it for you.'

The man replied, 'How long must I wait? It is quite chilly and I might catch cold.'[412]

A friend volunteered to build a shower room for 'Abdu'l-Bahá's use. After only three days, He asked the man when the project would be completed and then told this story.

157

The Rooster Did Not Crow but the Sun Rose

'When the mists and darkness of superstition and prejudice are dispersed, all will see the Sun aright and alike.'[413]   'Abdu'l-Bahá

In the chicken yard, the rooster was so ill that no one could count on his crowing the next morning. The hens were very worried that the sun wouldn't rise if the crowing of their lord and master did not summon it. The hens, you see, thought the sun came up only because the rooster crowed. The next day the sun cured them of their superstition. To be sure, the rooster was still too sick and too hoarse to crow, but the sun shone anyway; nothing bad affected its course.[414]

Despite superstition and dogmas, amidst all the scepticism and disbelief, the Manifestations of God emerge victorious and establish the divine principles.

158

This Bad Food Became Excellent a Few Days Later

'Serve ye the sovereigns of the world with utmost truthfulness and loyalty. Show obedience unto them and be their well-wishers.'[415]   'Abdu'l-Bahá

A king told his minister that eggplant was reported to be bad for one's health.

The minister said, 'Yes, it causes melancholy and is harmful to one's liver and nervous system.'

After some time the king said to the minister, 'I ate some eggplant, and it was very delicious.'

The minister responded, 'Yes, your majesty. It is indeed very good and has many beneficial effects.'

The king said, 'Was it not you who, not long ago, said bad things about eggplant?'

The minister answered, 'Yes, it was I. I happen to be your servant and not the servant of an eggplant.'[416]

'Abdu'l-Bahá was explaining to a questioner the origin of the saying 'I am the servant of the king not of an eggplant'.

159

The Tasty Dish Moved the Boundary

'But man hath perversely continued to serve his lustful appetites, and he would not content himself with simple foods.'[417]   'Abdu'l-Bahá

Once upon a time two men had a quarrel over a piece of land. It was a dispute over the boundary line. One of them invited the judge to his home for dinner. Afterwards the judge departed and changed the boundary line, taking a piece of land from the other. When the other one found this out, he invited the judge to his house for dinner and served him this dish ['mouthful of the judge', a fritter dipped in honey]. When the judge had eaten this delicious dish he went back, and as he had given the former man ten metres, he now reversed the boundary line and gave to the second one twenty metres, because the former had only served him eggs. When he was asked by this man, 'Why did you give me ten metres and then take twenty metres from me?' the judge replied: 'The first line was based upon the egg, but this one was based upon the mouthful of the judge.' So this dish received its name.[418]

'Abdu'l-Bahá told this story when this Turkish dish, 'mouthful of the judge', was served to the pilgrims in Haifa.

160

He Did Not Have Enough Fabric for All the Thieves

'And among the teachings of Bahá'u'lláh is voluntary sharing of one's property with others among mankind.'[419]   'Abdu'l-Bahá

Once a cloth merchant bought some fabric in Baghdad and was taking it to his own town to sell. On the way, he encountered some thieves. They took all the fabric from him and, using a spear, measured it and distributed it among themselves. Since there was not enough for every thief to receive a share, they started beating the trader, saying, 'Why didn't you bring enough?'

The trader responded, 'By God, I didn't expect to have so many customers with cash in hand. Otherwise, I would have brought much more.'[420]

Soroush, a gardener, presented 'Abdu'l-Bahá with some flowers. He immediately distributed them among the people who were with Him but they were quite a few and some did not receive any.

Bibliography

'Abdu'l-Bahá. *Foundations of World Unity.* Wilmette, IL: Bahá'í Publishing Trust, 1945.
— *Khiṭábát-i-'Abdu'l-Bahá.* Hofheim-Langenhain: Bahá'í-Verlag, 1984.
— *Memorials of the Faithful.* Wilmette, IL: Bahá'í Publishing Trust, 1971.
— *Muntakhabátí az Makátíb-i Ḥaḍrat-i 'Abdu'l-Bahá, vol. 3.* Hofheim-Langenhain: Bahá'í-Verlag, 1992.
— *Paris Talks.* London: Bahá'í Publishing Trust, 1967.
— *The Promulgation of Universal Peace.* Wilmette, IL: Bahá'í Publishing Trust, 1982.
— *The Secret of Divine Civilization.* Wilmette, IL: Bahá'í Publishing Trust, 1990.
— *Selections from the Writings of 'Abdu'l-Bahá.* Haifa: Bahá'í World Centre, 1978.
— *Some Answered Questions.* Wilmette, IL: Bahá'í Publishing Trust, 1981.
— *Tablets of Abdul-Baha Abbas.* Chicago: Bahá'í Publishing Society; vol. 1, 1909; vol. 2, 1915; vol. 3, 1916.
— *A Traveler's Narrative.* Wilmette, IL: Bahá'í Publishing Trust, 1980.
— *The Will and Testament of 'Abdu'l-Bahá.* Wilmette, IL: Bahá'í Publishing Trust, 1971.

Abdul Baha on Divine Philosophy. Boston: The Tudor Press, 1918.

'Abdu'l-Bahá in London. London: Bahá'í Publishing Trust, 1987.

Afnán, Abu'l-Qásim. *'Ahd-i A'lá Zindigáníy-i Ḥaḍrat-i Báb.* Oxford: Oneworld Publications, 2000.

Afrúkhtih, Yúnis. *Kháṭirát-i Nuh Sálih.* Los Angeles: Kalimát Press, 1983.

The Báb. *Selections from the Writings of the Báb.* Haifa: Bahá'í World Centre, 1976.

Bahá'í World Faith. Wilmette, IL: Bahá'í Publishing Trust, 2nd edn. 1976.

Bahá'u'lláh. *Epistle to the Son of the Wolf*. Wilmette, IL: Bahá'í Publishing Trust, 1988.
— *Gleanings from the Writings of Bahá'u'lláh*. Wilmette, IL: Bahá'í Publishing Trust, 1983.
— *The Hidden Words*. Wilmette, IL: Bahá'í Publishing Trust, 1990.
— *Kitáb-i-Íqán*. Wilmette, IL: Bahá'í Publishing Trust, 1989.
— *Prayers and Meditations*. Wilmette, IL: Bahá'í Publishing Trust, 1987.
— *The Proclamation of Bahá'u'lláh*. Haifa: Bahá'í World Centre, 1967.
— *The Seven Valleys and the Four Valleys*. Wilmette, IL: Bahá'í Publishing Trust, 1991.
— *The Summons of the Lord of Hosts: Tablets of Bahá'u'lláh*. Haifa: Bahá'í World Centre, 2002.
— *Tablets of Bahá'u'lláh revealed after the Kitáb-i-Aqdas*. Haifa: Bahá'í World Centre, 1978.

Balyuzi, H. M. *'Abdu'l-Bahá: The Centre of the Covenant of Bahá'u'lláh*. Oxford: George Ronald, 2nd edn. with minor corr. 1987.
— *Bahá'u'lláh, The King of Glory*. Oxford: George Ronald, 1980.

Blomfield, Lady [Sara Louise]. *The Chosen Highway*. Wilmette, IL: Bahá'í Publishing Trust, 1967.

Compilation of Compilations, The. Prepared by the Universal House of Justice 1963–1990. 2 vols. [Sydney]: Bahá'í Publications Australia, 1991.

Diary of Juliet Thompson, The. Los Angeles: Kalimát Press, 1983.

Directives from the Guardian. Compiled by Gertrude Garrida. New Delhi: Bahá'í Publishing Trust, 1973.

Gash, Andrew. *Stories from 'Star of the West'*, Mona Vale, N.S.W.: Bahá'í Publications Australia, 1985.

Grundy, Julia M. *Ten Days in the Light of 'Akká*. Wilmette, IL: Bahá'í Publishing Trust, 1979.

Ishráq Khávarí, 'Abdu'l-Ḥamid-i. *Má'idiy-i-Ásmání*. New Delhi: Bahá'í Publishing Trust, 1984.
— *Muḥáḍirát*. Hofheim: Bahá'í-Verlag, 1987.
— *Payám-i-Malakút*. New Delhi: Bahá'í Publishing Trust, 1986.
— *Raḥíq-i Makhtúm*. 2 vols. Tehran: Bahá'í Publishing Trust, 1973.

Ives, Howard Colby. *Portals to Freedom*. London: George Ronald, 1967.

Japan Will Turn Ablaze. Japan: Bahá'í Publishing Trust, 1974.

Khátirát-i Mírzá 'Isá Isfáhání. Unpublished, 1298 AH (1919 AD).

Latimer, George Orr. *The Light of the World*. Haifa, Palestine: n.p., 1920.

Makátíb-i-'Abdu'l-Bahá. Cairo: Kurdistan-il ilmiyyih, 1328 AH (1910 AD).

Mázandarání, Fáḍil. *Asráru'l-Áthár*. Five vols. Tehran: National Bahá'í Publishing Trust, 124–9 BE.

Mu'ayyad, Ḥabíb. *Khátirát-i-Ḥabíb*. Hofheim: Bahá'í-Verlag, 1998.

Payám-i-Ásmání. National Spiritual Assembly of France, 2001.

Payam-i-Bahá'í.

Pesechkian, N. *The Merchant and the Parrot: Mideastern Stories as Tools in Psychotherapy*. New York: Vantage Press, 1982.

Rosenberg, Ethel J. Pilgrim Notes taken at Haifa in February and March 1901. Unpublished.

Shoghi Effendi. *God Passes By*. Wilmette, IL: Bahá'í Publishing Trust, rev. edn. 1974.

Sohrab, Mirza Ahmad. *Abdul Baha in Egypt.* London: Rider & Co., no date.

Star of the West. rpt. Oxford: George Ronald, 1984.

Taherzadeh, Adib. *The Revelation of Bahá'u'lláh*, vol. 3. Oxford: George Ronald, 1983.

The Universal House of Justice. *Wellspring of Guidance.* Wilmette, IL: Bahá'í Publishing Trust, 1976.

Zarqání, Mírzá Maḥmúd-i-. *Badáyi'u'-Áthár.* 2 vols. Bombay: Paris Publishing House, vol. 1, 1914; vol. 2, 1921.

Notes and References

1. 'Abdu'l-Bahá, *Promulgation*, p. 186.
2. *Star of the West*, vol. 9, no. 18, pp. 207–8.
3. Bahá'u'lláh, *Hidden Words*, Persian no. 8.
4. A Sufi-like sect of Islam which originated in Turkey; a member of this sect.
5. Sohrab, *Abdul Baha in Egypt*, pp. 220–1.
6. Bahá'u'lláh, *Gleanings*, p. 10.
7. Mullá Muḥammad-'Alí, a distinguished believer from Qá'ín, a town in northeastern Iran.
8. Bahá'u'lláh's son, Mírzá Mihdí, who in 1870, while praying one evening on the roof of the prison, fell to his death.
9. 'Abdu'l-Bahá, *Memorials of the Faithful*, pp. 53–4.
10. 'Abdu'l-Bahá, *Selections*, p. 242.
11. A northern province of Iran, just south of the Caspian Sea.
12. *Star of the West*, vol. 13, no. 10, pp. 271–2.
13. Bahá'u'lláh, *Tablets*, p. 36.
14. 'Abdu'l-Bahá, *Promulgation*, pp. 426–7.
15. Bahá'u'lláh, *Gleanings*, p. 202.
16. 'Alí, Ḥasan and Ḥusayn were the first, second and third Imáms respectively. Fáṭimih was the daughter of the Prophet Muḥammad and the wife of Imám 'Alí.
17. This refers probably to one of the following verses 30:38 or 2:177, 215.
18. Translated and adapted from *Payám-i-Bahá'í*, 1997, no. 210, p. 17.
19. Bahá'u'lláh, in *Compilation*, p. 505.
20. Basra, a port and the second largest city in Iraq. It was called Balsora in the stories of the voyages of Sinbad.
21. *Star of the West*, vol. 13, no. 6, p. 151.
22. 'Abdu'l-Bahá, *Paris Talks*, p. 176.
23. *Star of the West*, vol. 9, no. 18, pp. 209–10.
24. Bahá'u'lláh, *Gleanings*, p. 297.
25. Translated and adapted from *Star of the West*, vol. 12, no. 3, p. 61 (Persian section).
26. Bahá'u'lláh, *Epistle to the Son of the Wolf*, p. 23.

27. 'Abdu'l-Bahá, *Memorials of the Faithful*, pp. 161–2.

28. 'Abdu'l-Bahá, in *Bahá'í World Faith*, p. 384.

29. Founder of the Afshár dynasty; he ruled Iran from 1736 to 1747.

30. Translated and adapted from Mu'ayyad, *Khátirát-i-Habíb*, vol. 1, p. 213.

31. 'Abdu'l-Bahá, in *Bahá'í World Faith*, p. 384.

32. All three were Abbasid caliphs. The Abbasid caliphs ruled at Baghdad from 750 to 1258.

33. The capital city of the Abbasid caliphs.

34. Translated and adapted from Mu'ayyad, *Khátirát-i-Habíb*, vol. 1, pp. 214–15.

35. 'Abdu'l-Bahá, *Paris Talks*, p. 65.

36. Monetary unit in Iran.

37. The dynasty which ruled Iran from 1794 to 1925. The ministries of the Báb, Bahá'u'lláh and 'Abdu'l-Bahá were during the reign of this despotic dynasty.

38. Translated and adapted from *Payám-i-Bahá'í*, 1997, no. 210, p. 18.

39. 'Abdu'l-Bahá, *Selections*, p. 294.

40. Jazira is the northern reaches of Mesopotamia, lying between the Tigris and Euphrates. Its King Harith the Lame was of the Ghassanid dynasty, which reached the peak of its power in the 6th century AD.

41. Translated and adapted from Mu'ayyad, *Khátirát-i-Habíb*, vol. 1, p. 36.

42. Bahá'u'lláh, *Gleanings*, p. 233.

43. Translated and adapted from Mu'ayyad, *Khátirát-i-Habíb*, vol. 1, p. 111.

44. Bahá'u'lláh, *Tablets*, p. 37.

45. The fifth Umayyad caliph, who ruled from 685 to 705. The Umayyad caliphs ruled at Damascus from 661 to 750 AD.

46. Translated and adapted from Mu'ayyad, *Khátirát-i-Habíb*, vol. 1, p. 184.

47. 'Abdu'l-Bahá, *Paris Talks*, p. 113.

48. A king of the Qájár dynasty who ruled Iran from 1797 to 1834.

49. People who live in Turkmenistan, a country in central Asia, bordering the Caspian Sea between Iran and Kazakhstan.

50. Poems by Jalál-i-Dín Rúmí, composed in six books some-time between 1246 and 1273.
51. Translated and adapted from Iṣhráq Khávarí, *Muḥáḍirát*, pp. 571–2.
52. Bahá'u'lláh, *Hidden Words*, Persian no. 76.
53. Adapted from *Star of the West*, vol. 13, no. 7, pp. 182–3 by Andrew Gash, in *Stories from 'Star of the West'*.
54. Bahá'u'lláh, *Gleanings*, p. 285.
55. Translated and adapted from Zarqání, *Badáyi'u'-Áthár*, vol. 1, p. 222.
56. Bahá'u'lláh, *Hidden Words*, Persian no. 37.
57. Adapted from *Star of the West*, vol. 13, no. 7, p. 183 by Andrew Gash, in *Stories from 'Star of the West'*.
58. 'Abdu'l-Bahá, *Promulgation*, p. 174.
59. Adapted from *Star of the West*, vol. 13, no. 7, pp. 183–4 by Andrew Gash, in *Stories from 'Star of the West'*.
60. Bahá'u'lláh, *Hidden Words*, Arabic no. 48.
61. Traditional lamentation gathering in commemoration of Imám Ḥusayn's martyrdom.
62. Second Umayyad caliph (680–3), responsible for Imám Ḥusayn's martyrdom.
63. 'Alí Akbar and Qásim are members of Ḥusayn's family.
64. Translated and adapted from Mu'ayyad, *Kháṭirát-i-Ḥabíb*, vol. 1, pp. 150–1.
65. Bahá'u'lláh, *Tablets*, p. 156.
66. Some Muslims believe that if they touch unclean things, or certain people (atheists or people of different faiths), they become unclean themselves.
67. *Star of the West*, vol. 9, no. 18, p. 207.
68. *Star of the West*, vol. 9, no. 10, pp. 108–9.
69. Bahá'u'lláh, *Gleanings*, p. 305.
70. *'Abdu'l-Bahá in London*, p. 60.
71. 'Abdu'l-Bahá, *Promulgation*, p. 98.
72. 'Abdu'l-Bahá, in Ives, *Portals to Freedom*, p. 196.
73. 'Abdu'l-Bahá, *Tablets*, vol. 2, p. 445.
74. Translated and adapted from Afrúkhtih, *Kháṭirát-i Nuh Sálih*, p. 371.
75. Bahá'u'lláh, *Hidden Words*, Persian no. 24.
76. The art of determining character or personal characteristics

from the form or features of the body, especially the face.

77. Translated and adapted from Afrúkhtih, *Khátirát-i Nuh Sálih*, pp. 366–8.

78. The Báb, *Selections*, p. 202.

79. Translated and adapted from Zarqání, *Badáyi'u'-Áthár*, vol. 2, p. 178.

80. 'Abdu'l-Bahá, *Selections*, p. 121.

81. Adapted from Balyuzi, *'Abdu'l-Bahá*, pp. 30–1.

82. 'Abdu'l-Bahá, *Secret of Divine Civilization*, p. 96.

83. Grundy, *Ten Days in the Light of 'Akká*, pp. 13–14.

84. Bahá'u'lláh, *Tablets*, p. 155.

85. Early believers in Islam and companions of the Prophet Muḥammad.

86. Translated and adapted from Ishráq Khávarí, *Muḥáḍirát*, pp. 126–7.

87. Bahá'u'lláh, *Gleanings*, p. 276.

88. Translated and adapted from Zarqání, *Badáyi'u'-Áthár*, vol. 1, p. 271.

89. Bahá'u'lláh, *Hidden Words*, Arabic no. 32.

90. Sohrab, *Abdul Baha in Egypt*, pp. 217–18.

91. 'Abdu'l-Bahá, *Will and Testament*, p. 23.

92. Commander of the army of Mázindarán and a brother of Muḥammad Sháh, the Qájár monarch.

93. Translated and adapted from *Star of the West*, vol. 12, no. 5, p. 109 (Persian section).

94. Bahá'u'lláh, *Hidden Words*, Arabic no. 47.

95. Qur'án 3:193

96. 'Abdu'l-Bahá, in Blomfield, *Chosen Highway*, pp. 196–7.

97. Bahá'u'lláh, *Gleanings*, p. 246.

98. He was Iran's Prime Minister during the reign of Náṣiri'd-Dín Sháh. It was he who ordered the execution of the Báb.

99. *Star of the West*, vol. 3, no. 11, p. 6.

100. ibid.

101. Bahá'u'lláh, *Hidden Words*, Arabic no. 46.

102. *Diary of Juliet Thompson*, p. 319.

103. Bahá'u'lláh, *Hidden Words*, Persian no. 14.

104. Translated and adapted from Zarqání, *Badáyi'u'-Áthár*, vol. 1, p. 29.

105. 'Abdu'l-Bahá, *Promulgation*, p. 109.

106. 'Abdu'l-Bahá, _Khiṭábát-i-'Abdu'l-Bahá_, pp. 16–17.

107. Bahá'u'lláh, _Gleanings_, p. 236.

108. A city in southeast Turkey, on the Tigris.

109. At that time, all the kings of the Muslim world were under the general authority of the caliphs.

110. Translated and adapted from _Payám-i-Bahá'í_, 1998, no. 218, pp. 18–19.

111. Bahá'u'lláh, _Hidden Words_, Arabic no. 23.

112. A Persian king of the Ghaznavid dynasty who ruled from 977 to 997.

113. _Star of the West_, vol. 9, no. 18, pp. 204–5.

114. Translated and adapted from Ishráq Khávarí, _Má'idiy-i-Ásmání_, vol. 5, p. 244.

115. 'Abdu'l-Bahá, _Paris Talks_, p. 72.

116. Translated and adapted from Zarqání, _Badáyi'u'-Áthár_, vol. 1, p. 185.

117. Bahá'u'lláh, _Hidden Words_, Persian no. 44.

118. Pilgrim Notes of Ethel J. Rosenberg, taken at Haifa in February and March 1901, p. 1.

119. John 8:11

120. 'Abdu'l-Bahá, in _Bahá'í World Faith_, p. 412.

121. A Persian king of the Sassanid dynasty who ruled from 531 to 579.

122. 'Abdu'l-Bahá, _Secret of Divine Civilization_, pp. 68–9.

123. Bahá'u'lláh, _Gleanings_, pp. 233–4.

124. A Seljukid king who ruled Iran from 1096 to 1157.

125. A city in northeastern Iran.

126. Qur'án 27:34

127. ibid.

128. Translated and adapted from _Payám-i-Bahá'í_, 1998, no. 218, p. 18.

129. 'Abdu'l-Bahá, _Tablets_, vol. 1, p. 148.

130. Translated and adapted from Mu'ayyad, _Kháṭirát-i-Ḥabíb_, vol. 1, p. 194.

131. Bahá'u'lláh, _Tablets_, p. 164.

132. 'Abdu'l-Bahá, _Foundations of World Unity_, pp. 41–2.

133. Bahá'u'lláh, _Epistle to the Son of the Wolf_, p. 24.

134. A tyrannical commander during the reign of 'Abdu'l-Malik ibn Marwán, the Umayyad caliph.

135. Translated and adapted from Zarqání, *Badáyi'u'-Áthár*, vol. 2, p. 108.
136. Bahá'u'lláh, *Gleanings*, p. 296.
137. Napoleon I, Emperor of France from 1804 to 1815.
138. It was a common practice to use fine soil to dry wet ink.
139. Translated and adapted from Mu'ayyad, *Khátirát-i-Habíb*, p. 190.
140. Bahá'u'lláh, *Gleanings*, p. 211.
141. Translated and adapted from *Star of the West*, vol. 11, no. 19, p. 341 (Persian section).
142. 'Abdu'l-Bahá, *Will and Testament*, p. 13.
143. *Star of the West*, vol. 8, no. 11, p. 143.
144. 'Abdu'l-Bahá, *Promulgation*, p. 216.
145. Translated and adapted from Mu'ayyad, *Khátirát-i-Habíb*, vol. 1, p. 226.
146. Bahá'u'lláh, *Epistle to the Son of the Wolf*, p. 29.
147. *Star of the West*, vol. 11, no. 16, pp. 269–70.
148. Bahá'u'lláh, *Gleanings*, p. 179.
149. 'Abdu'l-Bahá, *Promulgation*, p. 43.
150. 'Abdu'l-Bahá, *Selections*, p. 267.
151. *'Abdu'l-Bahá in London*, pp. 63–4.
152. ibid. p. 63.
153. Bahá'u'lláh, *Tablets*, pp. 155–6.
154. 'Abdu'l-Bahá, *Promulgation*, pp. 33–4.
155. 'Abdu'l-Bahá, *Tablets*, vol. 1, p. 45.
156. Translated and adapted from Mu'ayyad, *Khátirát-i-Habíb*, vol. 1, p. 284.
157. 'Abdu'l-Bahá, *Selections*, p. 169.
158. Bahá'u'lláh, *Gleanings*, p. 136.
159. Translated and adapted from 'Abdu'l-Bahá, *Khitábát-i-'Abdu'l-Bahá*, pp. 417–20.
160. 'Abdu'l-Bahá, *Promulgation*, p. 200.
161. *Diary of Juliet Thompson*, p. 91.
162. Bahá'u'lláh, *Tablets*, p. 168.
163. 'Abdu'l-Bahá, *Promulgation*, p. 73.
164. ibid. p. 421.
165. Emperor Tiberias, who ruled from 14 to 17 AD.
166. Translated and adapted from Zarqání, *Badáyi'u'-Áthár*, vol. 2, p. 37.

167. 'Abdu'l-Bahá, *Some Answered Questions*, p. 113.
168. Bishop of Constantinople from 398 to 407.
169. Translated and adapted from 'Abdu'l-Bahá, *Khiṭábát-i-'Abdu'l-Bahá*, p. 739.
170. 'Abdu'l-Bahá, *Selections*, p. 46.
171. Latimer, *Light of the World*, pp. 76–7.
172. 'Abdu'l-Bahá, *Promulgation*, p. 361.
173. 'Abdu'l-Bahá, *Secret of Divine Civilization*, pp. 46–51.
174. ibid. p. 46.
175. Bahá'u'lláh, *Gleanings*, p. 26.
176. An enemy of Muḥammad and the commander of the armies who fought the Muslims in the Battle of Badr. Subsequent to the conquest of Mecca by the Muslims, he professed his belief in Islam.
177. A region in southeastern Arabia which contains the sacred cities of Mecca and Medina.
178. Translated and adapted from *Star of the West*, vol. 2, no. 7, pp. 8–9 (Persian section).
179. 'Abdu'l-Bahá, *Selections*, p. 281.
180. The first caliph
181. Translated and adapted from Zarqání, *Badáyi'u'-Áthár*, vol. 1, p. 227.
182. Qur'án 31:33
183. Dissemblers who paid lip service to Islam but decried it at every opportunity.
184. Title of a Persian king in the Sassanid dynasty.
185. Translated and adapted from Zarqání, *Badáyi'u'-Áthár*, vol. 2, p. 156; Mu'ayyad, *Khátirát-i-Ḥabíb*, vol. 1, p. 19.
186. The Báb, *Selections*, p. 132.
187. Muḥammad's tribe, whose members severely persecuted Him and His followers.
188. His name was Nu'aym ibn Mas'úd – he was a new convert to Islam and not many knew this.
189. Translated and adapted from Zarqání, *Badáyi'u'-Áthár*, vol. 2, p. 130.
190. Bahá'u'lláh, *Gleanings*, p. 215.
191. The sixth caliph of the Fatamid dynasty; he ruled from 996 to 1021. He is considered to be the founder of the Druze, a sect of Islam.

192. Translated and adapted from Ishráq Khávarí, *Muḥáḍirát*, pp. 188–9.

193. Bahá'u'lláh, *Gleanings*, p. 30.

194. *Diary of Juliet Thompson*, p. 91.

195. 'Abdu'l-Bahá, *Selections*, p. 241.

196. Translated and adapted from Mu'ayyad, *Khátirát-i-Ḥabíb*, vol. i, p. 28.

197. 'Abdu'l-Bahá, *Promulgation*, p. 152.

198. *Star of the West*, vol. 14, no. 6, p. 181.

199. 'Abdu'l-Bahá, *Promulgation*, p. 466.

200. A port city in southern Iran

201. Translated and adapted from Afnán, *'Ahd-i A'lá Zindigáníy-i Haḍrat-i Báb*, pp. 41–2.

202. 'Abdu'l-Bahá, *Promulgation*, p. 257.

203. Pilgrimage notes of Louis Gregory, 1997, p. 17.

204. 'Abdu'l-Bahá, *Paris Talks*, pp. 61–2.

205. For many years Prime Minister of Iran during the reign of Náṣiri'd-Dín Sháh.

206. Qur'án 6:59

207. Qur'án 19:18. 'Taqí' means 'God-fearing'.

208. Qur'án 3:183. Qurbán means 'sacrifice' or 'offering'.

209. Taherzadeh, *Revelation of Bahá'u'lláh*, vol. 3, pp. 245–6.

210. Bahá'u'lláh, *Gleanings*, p. 139.

211. A celebrated Persian calligrapher

212. Supplications of the Imám 'Alí

213. Translated and adapted from Ishráq Khávarí, *Rahíq-i Makhtúm*, vol. 2, p. 257.

214. Bahá'u'lláh, *Kitáb-i-Iqán*, pp. 250–1.

215. Translated and adapted from Afnán, *'Ahd-i A'lá Zindigáníy-i Haḍrat-i Báb*, pp. 509–10.

216. Bahá'u'lláh, *Prayers and Meditations*, p. 19.

217. Doctors of Islamic law

218. A mischief-maker and a bitter enemy of Bahá'u'lláh while He was residing in Baghdad.

219. A town north of Baghdad, where the seventh and the ninth Imáms are buried.

220. Head of the Shí'í community, a pious man who was friendly towards the Faith.

221. Balyuzi, *King of Glory*, pp. 143–4.

222. Bahá'u'lláh, *Kitáb-i-Íqán*, p. 37.

223. A mischief-maker and a bitter enemy of Bahá'u'lláh while He was residing in Baghdad.

224. A book by the great Andalusian mystic Shaykh Muhyi'd-Dín ibn al-'Arabí.

225. Fusus al-Hikam: Another book by Shaykh Muhyi'd-Dín. Translated and adapted from Zarqání, *Badáyi'u'-Áthár*, vol. 1, p. 175.

226. 'Abdu'l-Bahá, *Promulgation*, p. 175.

227. Qur'án 2:255. This verse is usually recited by Muslims for protection.

228. Translated and adapted from 'Abdu'l-Bahá, *Khitábát-i-'Abdu'l-Bahá*, p. 752.

229. Qur'án 3:180

230. 'Abdu'l-Bahá, *Some Answered Questions*, pp. 28–30.

231. Bahá'u'lláh, *Gleanings*, p. 206.

232. A follower of the Shaykhí school of Shí'í Islam which was founded by Shaykh Ahmad and carried on by Siyyid Kázim, forerunners of the Báb.

233. Translated and adapted from Afnán, *'Ahd-i A'lá Zindigáníy-i Hadrat-i Báb*, pp. 77–8.

234. Bahá'u'lláh, *Gleanings*, p. 12.

235. Sohrab, *Abdul Baha in Egypt*, p. 184.

236. Bahá'u'lláh, *Tablets*, pp. 259–60.

237. Sohrab, *Abdul Baha in Egypt*, pp. 169–70.

238. 'Abdu'l-Bahá, *Promulgation*, p. 214.

239. 'Abdu'l-Bahá, *Memorials of the Faithful*, pp. 91–3.

240. 'Abdu'l-Bahá, *Selections*, p. 16.

241. Expounder of Islamic law. His name was Shaykh 'Alíy-i-Mírí.

242. Translated and adapted from Zarqání, *Badáyi'u'-Áthár*, vol. 2, pp. 197–8.

243. Bahá'u'lláh, *Tablets*, p. 156.

244. The capital city of Azerbaijan

245. Translated and adapted from *Star of the West*, vol. 12, no. 6, p. 126 (Persian section).

246. Bahá'u'lláh, *Prayers and Meditations*, p. 262.

247. Mírzá Ja'far-i-Yazdí, a very learned believer from Yazd who went to Baghdad and from there accompanied Bahá'u'lláh

to Constantinople, Adrianople and eventually 'Akká.

248. 'Abdu'l-Bahá, *Memorials of the Faithful*, pp. 157–8.
249. 'Abdu'l-Bahá, *Tablets*, vol. 1, p. 24.
250. *Diary of Juliet Thompson*, p. 171.
251. Bahá'u'lláh, *Summons*, para. 114.
252. Translated and adapted from *Khátirát-i Mírzá 'Isá Isfáhání*, p. 4.
253. 'Abdu'l-Bahá, *Tablets*, vol. 1, p. 106.
254. Latimer, *Light of the World*, p. 44.
255. Bahá'u'lláh, *Tablets*, p. 234.
256. Translated and adapted from Zarqání, *Badáyi'u'-Áthár*, vol. 2, p. 173.
257. 'Abdu'l-Bahá, in *Japan Will Turn Ablaze*, pp. 21–2.
258. Translated and adapted from Zarqání, *Badáyi'u'-Áthár*, vol. 2, p. 308.
259. Bahá'u'lláh, *Kitáb-i-Aqdas*, para. 40.
260. The governor of Beirut who held Syria in his grasp.
261. Imám 'Alí
262. Translated and adapted from Zarqání, *Badáyi'u'-Áthár*, vol. 2, p. 112.
263. Bahá'u'lláh, *Gleanings*, p. 162.
264. *Diary of Juliet Thompson*, p. 179.
265. Bahá'u'lláh, *Hidden Words*, Arabic no. 57.
266. Translated and adapted from Zarqání, *Badáyi'u'-Áthár*, vol. 2, p. 71.
267. Bahá'u'lláh, *Gleanings*, p. 220.
268. Expounder of Islamic Law. The Mufti pronounces judgement on points of jurisprudence.
269. Translated and adapted from *Khátirát-i Mírzá 'Isá Isfáhání*, pp. 18–21.
270. 'Abdu'l-Bahá, *Selections*, p. 129.
271. Translated and adapted from Zarqání, *Badáyi'u'-Áthár*, vol. 2, pp. 149–50.
272. 'Abdu'l-Bahá, *Promulgation*, p. 129.
273. Translated and adapted from 'Abdu'l-Bahá, *Khitábát-i-'Abdu'l-Bahá*, p. 712.
274. Bahá'u'lláh, *Epistle to the Son of the Wolf*, p. 61.
275. Sohrab, *Abdul Baha in Egypt*, pp. 312–13.
276. Bahá'u'lláh, *Gleanings*, p. 213.

277. 'Abdu'l-Bahá, *Memorials of the Faithful*, pp. 67–9.
278. 'Abdu'l-Bahá, *Selections*, pp. 198–9.
279. *Star of the West*, vol. 9, no. 18, p. 208.
280. Bahá'u'lláh, *Gleanings*, pp. 56–7.
281. 'Abdu'l-Bahá, *Paris Talks*, p. 46.
282. 'Abdu'l-Bahá, *Promulgation*, p. 142.
283. Translated and adapted from Mu'ayyad, *Khátirát-i-Habíb*, vol. 1, p. 11.
284. 'Abdu'l-Bahá, *Tablets*, vol. 2, p. 423.
285. *Star of the West*, vol. 4, no. 6, p. 105.
286. The Báb, *Selections*, p. 69.
287. *Star of the West*, vol. 9, no. 2, p. 17.
288. 'Abdu'l-Bahá, *Tablets*, vol. 1, p. 38.
289. Unit of distance, about three to four miles, the distance a laden mule walks in one hour.
290. *Star of the West*, vol. 4, no. 6, p. 104.
291. ibid.
292. Bahá'u'lláh, *Tablets*, p. 139.
293. Translated and adapted from Mu'ayyad, *Khátirát-i-Habíb*, vol. 1, p. 225.
294. Bahá'u'lláh, *Gleanings*, p. 278.
295. *Star of the West*, vol. 9, no. 3, p. 36.
296. 'Abdu'l-Bahá, *Promulgation*, p. 249.
297. ibid. p. 250; *Star of the West*, vol. 3, no. 18, p. 7.
298. 'Abdu'l-Bahá, *Promulgation*, p. 249.
299. 'Abdu'l-Bahá, *Tablets*, vol. 2, p. 320.
300. Possibly, a 13th-century Sufi leader
301. Translated and adapted from Zarqání, *Badáyi'u'-Áthár*, vol. 2. pp. 61–2.
302. Bahá'u'lláh, *Hidden Words*, Arabic no. 49.
303. Translated and adapted from Mu'ayyad, *Khátirát-i-Habíb*, vol. 1, p. 53.
304. Bahá'u'lláh, *Tablets*, p. 242.
305. *Star of the West*, vol. 9, no. 3, p. 36.
306. Bahá'u'lláh, *Kitáb-i-Íqán*, pp. 195–6.
307. Translated and adapted from Zarqání, *Badáyi'u'-Áthár*, vol. 2, p. 218.
308. 'Abdu'l-Bahá, *Tablets*, vol. 1, p. 223.
309. *Star of the West*, vol. 4, no. 12, p. 205.

310. 'Abdu'l-Bahá, *Tablets*, vol. 1, p. 222.
311. A city in the central part of Iran
312. 'Abdu'l-Bahá, *Traveler's Narrative*, p. 21.
313. ibid.
314. Bahá'u'lláh, *Proclamation*, p. 79.
315. Manúchihr Khán, the governor of Isfahan
316. His name was Muḥammad-Mihdí and was called Safíhu'l-'Ulamá.
317. Translated and adapted from Zarqání, *Badáyi'u'-Áthár*, vol. 2, p. 158.
318. Bahá'u'lláh, *Gleanings*, p. 72.
319. A mountainous township which lies about 32 miles west of Hamadán, in western Iran. Its winters are extremely cold and harsh.
320. Translated and adapted from Mu'ayyad, *Khátirát-i-Habíb*, vol. 1, p. 18.
321. 'Abdu'l-Bahá, *Tablets*, p. 221.
322. Probably, the Viceroy and Páshá of Egypt, 1805–49.
323. *Star of the West*, vol. 9, no. 18, p. 210.
324. 'Abdu'l-Bahá, *Selections*, p. 258.
325. *Star of the West*, vol. 9, no. 18, p. 210.
326. 'Abdu'l-Bahá, *Will and Testament*, p. 9.
327. An ambitious and deceitful individual who was first a prominent Bahá'í teacher but later broke the Covenant during the ministry of 'Abdu'l-Bahá.
328. This conceited man played on the similarity of Bahá'u'lláh's title, Jamál-i-Mubárak, with that of his own name, Jamál.
329. Translated and adapted from Mu'ayyad, *Khátirát-i-Habíb*, vol. 1, p. 22.
330. Bahá'u'lláh, *Hidden Words*, Persian no. 13.
331. Translated and adapted from Mu'ayyad, *Khátirát-i-Habíb*, vol. 1, p. 241.
332. 'Abdu'l-Bahá, *Some Answered Questions*, p. 92.
333. Translated and adapted from *Star of the West*, vol. 11, no. 19, p. 341 (Persian section).
334. Bahá'u'lláh, *Gleanings*, p. 291.
335. Sohrab, *Abdul Baha in Egypt*, pp. 218–19.
336. Bahá'u'lláh, *Tablets*, p. 24.

337. *Diary of Juliet Thompson*, p. 56.
338. 'Abdu'l-Bahá, in *Bahá'í World Faith*, p. 365.
339. A Muslim theologian and mystic, born 1058 and died 1111.
340. Friday Mosque in Shiraz, Iran
341. Qur'án, 39:54
342. Translated and adapted from *Makátíb-i-'Abdu'l-Bahá*, vol. 2, pp. 56–7.
343. Bahá'u'lláh, *Tablets*, p. 155.
344. *Diary of Juliet Thompson*, pp. 59–60.
345. 'Abdu'l-Bahá, *Promulgation*, p. 216.
346. *Star of the West*, vol. 7, no. 9, pp. 82–3.
347. 'Abdu'l-Bahá, *Selections*, p. 302.
348. 'Abdu'l-Bahá, *Promulgation*, pp. 135–6.
349. ibid. p. 175.
350. 'Abdu'l-Bahá, in *Star of the West*, vol. 3, no. 8, p. 20. See also 'Abdu'l-Bahá, *Promulgation*, p. 282.
351. 'Abdu'l-Bahá, *Promulgation*, p. 74.
352. Translated and adapted from Ishráq Khávarí, *Payám-i-Malakút*, p. 241; Ishráq Khávarí, *Má'idiy-i-Ásmání*, vol. 5, pp. 249–50.
353. Bahá'u'lláh, *Hidden Words*, Persian no. 76.
354. 'Abdu'l-Bahá, *Memorials of the Faithful*, p. 200.
355. 'Abdu'l-Bahá, *Selections*, p. 320.
356. The Báb's distinguished disciple who, according to Shoghi Effendi, was 'the most preeminent figure to enlist under the banner of the [Bábí] Faith'. Shoghi Effendi, *God Passes By*, p. 50.
357. A faithful disciple of the Báb and Bahá'u'lláh.
358. Translated and adapted from Zarqání, *Badáyi'u'-Áthár*, vol. 1, p. 280.
359. Bahá'u'lláh, *Hidden Words*, Persian no. 37.
360. Translated and adapted from Afnán, *'Ahd-i A'lá Zindigáníy-i Ḥaḍrat-i Báb*, pp. 595–6.
361. 'Abdu'l-Bahá, *Selections*, p. 202.
362. 'Abdu'l-Bahá, *Memorials of the Faithful*, pp. 41–2.
363. The Báb, *Selections*, p. 214.
364. The day of Imám Ḥusayn's martyrdom, a day of mourning.
365. Translated and adapted from Ishráq Khávarí, *Muḥáḍirát*, pp. 120–2.

366. Bahá'u'lláh, *Gleanings*, p. 215.
367. Sydney Sprague, an American Bahá'í who was a pioneer in India.
368. Balyuzi, *'Abdu'l-Bahá*, p. 371.
369. Bahá'u'lláh, *Tablets*, p. 165.
370. Translated and adapted from Ishráq Khávarí, *Payám-i-Malakút*, p. 40.
371. Bahá'u'lláh, *Gleanings*, pp. 249–50.
372. *Star of the West*, vol. 9, no. 18, p. 211. Another version of this story can be found in 'Abdu'l-Bahá, *Promulgation*, p. 248.
373. 'Abdu'l-Bahá, *Selections*, p. 301.
374. *Star of the West*, vol. 7, no. 9, p. 81.
375. ibid. pp. 79–81.
376. Bahá'u'lláh, *Tablets*, p. 127.
377. In Arabic *'ayn* is the word for eye but in Turkish it means bear. Latimer, *Light of the World*, p. 40.
378. Bahá'u'lláh, *Hidden Words*, Persian no. 8.
379. *Star of the West*, vol. 2, no. 4, p. 4.
380. 'Abdu'l-Bahá, in *Compilation*, vol. 2, p. 74.
381. *Diary of Juliet Thompson*, p. 81.
382. Bahá'u'lláh, *Gleanings*, p. 250.
383. Translated and adapted from Zarqání, *Badáyi'u'-Áthár*, vol. 2, p. 108.
384. Bahá'u'lláh, *Tablets*, p. 66.
385. Translated and adapted from Mu'ayyad, *Khátirát-i-Habíb*, vol. 1, p. 133.
386. Bahá'u'lláh, *Gleanings*, p. 188.
387. Reported words of 'Abdu'l-Bahá, 'Diary of Ahmad Sohrab', 5 August 1913, in *Star of the West*, vol. 9, no. 18, pp. 211–12.
388. 'Abdu'l-Bahá, *Promulgation*, p. 287.
389. The first Umayyad caliph, who ruled from 661 to 680.
390. Translated and adapted from *Khátirát-i-Mírzá Isá Isfáhání*, pp. 11–12.
391. 'Abdu'l-Bahá, *Promulgation*, p. 433.
392. Qur'án 89:7
393. A mythical Arab king at the time of the prophet Húd.
394. Translated and adapted from Zarqání, *Badáyi'u'-Áthár*, vol. 2, p. 185.
395. Bahá'u'lláh, *Gleanings*, p. 265.

396. Translated and adapted from *Star of the West*, vol. 11, no. 19, p. 341 (Persian section).

397. Bahá'u'lláh, *Hidden Words*, Persian no. 64.

398. Translated and adapted from Mu'ayyad, *Kháṭirát-i-Ḥabíb*, vol. 1, p. 185.

399. 'Abdu'l-Bahá, *Tablets*, vol. 1, p. 45.

400. *Star of the West*, vol. 5, no. 8, p. 116.

401. ibid.

402. Bahá'u'lláh, *Gleanings*, p. 207.

403. *Star of the West*, vol. 9, no. 18, p. 206.

404. Bahá'u'lláh, in *Bahá'í World Faith*, p. 171.

405. Philosopher, mathematician and astronomer, 1201–74.

406. Translated and adapted from Mu'ayyad, *Kháṭirát-i-Ḥabíb*, vol. 1, p. 262.

407. Bahá'u'lláh, *Tablets*, pp. 51–2.

408. *Star of the West*, vol. 9, no. 18, p. 210.

409. Bahá'u'lláh, in *Bahá'í World Faith*, p. 206.

410. Translated and adapted from Mu'ayyad, *Kháṭirát-i-Ḥabíb*, vol. 1, p. 34.

411. Bahá'u'lláh, *Seven Valleys*, p. 5.

412. Translated and adapted from Afrúkhtih, *Kháṭirát-i Nuh Sálih*, p. 361.

413. 'Abdu'l-Bahá, *Promulgation*, p. 79.

414. Peseschkian, *The Merchant and the Parrot*, p. 53.

415. 'Abdu'l-Bahá, *Will and Testament*, p. 15.

416. Translated and adapted from Mázandarání, *Asráru'l-Áthár*, p. 22.

417. 'Abdu'l-Bahá, *Selections*, p. 152.

418. Latimer, *Light of the World*, p. 67.

419. 'Abdu'l-Bahá, *Selections*, p. 302.

420. Translated and adapted from *Kháṭirát-i Mírzá 'Isá Iṣfáhání*, p. 17.